Hidden Witness
A Forest Glen Suspense

Bettie Boswell

www.MtZionRidgePress.com

Mt Zion Ridge Press LLC
295 Gum Springs Rd, NW
Georgetown, TN 37366

https://www.mtzionridgepress.com

ISBN 13: 978-1-962862-74-5

Published in the United States of America
Publication Date: May 15, 2025

Editor-In-Chief: Michelle Levigne
Executive Editor: Tamera Lynn Kraft

Cover art design by Tamera Lynn Kraft
Cover Art Copyright by Mt Zion Ridge Press LLC © 2025

Chapter One

They said confession was good for the soul. Winifred Grimsley, also known as Miss Freddie to her art students in remote southwestern Virginia, wasn't so sure at the moment. The past had finally caught up with her. She'd confessed her transgressions to Graham, the FBI man waiting for reinforcements, in her front room. Since then, worry about her future consumed her. A frowning African mask from her extensive travels hung on the wall, condemning her for past mistakes.

In the meantime, she gave her long lost protégé Amber Whitney a quick hug. The young thirty-something woman now suffered from fallout created by MAX Enterprises and Freddie's choices. Amber's father ran the company before his untimely demise. Miss Freddie had escaped the company's criminal involvement by accepting a payoff years ago to stay silent. Now she faced the law and possibly the loss of her precious teaching career.

"I'm sorry, Amber. If I'd made a different choice, you wouldn't be running for your life with a lone federal agent for protection."

A loud knock shook the front door, making Freddie step away from Amber. Two new men entered. She stared in disbelief as Graham introduced his boss, Kent Russell and another agent whose name she didn't catch as shock overtook her senses.

Miss Freddie stared at the man from her past and swallowed. If she could have conjured up her worst nightmare, it wouldn't have matched the fierce anger that flashed across Kent Russell's rugged face. He'd aged well, but wore a frown. The storm clouds gathering in his narrowed gray eyes threatened to erupt into an explosion of thunder and lightning, raining hail or sleet down onto her head. She deserved his wrath, but leaving years ago was for his protection. She'd left him without a hint of the trouble that would have followed them both if she'd stayed.

Her lifted chin broke the connection. She nodded to the other agent and watched Kent with her side vision. His gaze searched the room. He probably looked for something to throw or hit, if his clenched hands were any indication. She'd furnished her small home with a love of art and beauty. Pieces from around the world covered her walls and shelves. She hoped he could see she'd done well on her own.

A thought whispered across her heart. What would her life be like if she hadn't been alone? A whiff of mossy aftershave entered her nose, reminding her of the relationship they'd once shared.

"Winifred Grimsley. It's been a long time." Not Winnie or Freddie, just a tight rendition of her first and last names spoken through a clamped jaw. Her heart sank. What had happened to the pleasant man from her past? She'd pay for her history with him unless they could come to some kind of truce.

"Kent, I..."

He leaned closer. "I don't need to hear your excuses, not now, not ever." His harsh whisper brushed its way into her ear in a voice that those around her wouldn't be able to make out. He shook his head as if to clear his thoughts and then stared at her. "It seems you've gotten yourself into quite a predicament. This time you won't escape to who knows where until we have your testimony against MAX Enterprises. You will answer to me for everything." He raised his dark eyebrows and stared at her.

His look conveyed she'd answer for more than she wanted to talk about. She inclined her head to acknowledge hearing his words, unsure whether she could form an intelligible answer. Instead, she focused on a pastoral painting she'd collected in France, trying to calm the storm whirling in her mind.

A shudder ran down her spine before she stalked away toward her kitchen, which Amber's Agent Graham asked to use as a conference area. The group of FBI agents filling her house followed her. The clumping of Kent's western boots led the pounding steps treading behind her on hardwood floors.

Kent had always preferred cowboy footwear. Sweet memories flooded her mind. Long ago, his cowboy boots had rested on a battered footstool next to her black riding boots. They'd munched popcorn and watched old black and white movies before he headed home, after sharing a chaste kiss. The sweet recollection painted a picture of lost friendship and more. She wondered if he still rode. At one time he'd dreamed of being a mounted policeman patrolling a city park.

Her thoughts headed down a different trail as she removed remnants of her last meal from the table and pulled a lidded crock labeled 'cookies' in fanciful script from the counter. It held enough chocolate-chip cookies to feed her unexpected guests. She sighed inwardly as she remembered Kent's penchant for that exact dessert. Freddie had baked the treats earlier in the week. She'd not planned on entertaining a house full of people, especially not him. Maybe her moist cookies would soften his attitude. The scent of chocolate wafted through the kitchen when she lifted the lid of her decorative cookie container.

Kent might not even like chocolate chips anymore. He didn't seem to care for anyone right now. His frowning gaze swept across his agents and Amber, who joined them at the table. Kent's attitude proved time changed people, places, and things.

"These look delicious, Miss Freddie." Amber offered napkins to the men sitting around the butcher block table.

Kent snorted.

Freddie stomped from the room.

She went back to her office and chose to concentrate on contacting Human Resources about getting a substitute. She didn't want to give up her time with her students, but neither did she want her little magpies to be in danger because of her past. She had some videos on file for a substitute to use in her absence or for a classroom teacher to share if no sub became available.

Freddie turned and stared out the window behind her desk. The peace of the mountains in the distance called her as she lifted up a prayer to the Lord for forgiveness. Kent might never forgive her, but her fellow teacher, Mary, had led her to a renewal of her childhood faith. She'd been active in church for several years now and knew where to seek peace.

After several attempts at writing her absence request, she finally called her time off a family emergency and hoped that would suffice. Her bank of sick days grew each year due to rare use. The school staff would be surprised about her missing work. Little did they know her absence would ensure their safety.

She pulled out a piece of scrap paper and started making a list of half-completed projects needing an explanation. After transferring the list of directions and the video files to the online substitute drive, she hit send. Now the only magpie she needed to worry about was Amber.

The sweet young woman who sat at Miss Freddie's feet twenty-five years ago as a seven-year-old had certainly changed. Amber had grown from a quiet child into a beautiful and talented woman. The boss's neglected child had craved every moment with her 'Miss Freddie' as they did craft projects together in a busy office where Freddie worked as a secretary.

Amber now displayed a gift for creating artistic jewelry, which her father, unfortunately, used to hide secrets related to one of his schemes. FBI Agent Graham had traveled with Amber to retrieve a hidden electronic device in jewelry Max sent secretly to Freddie. Miss Freddie also held a few other secrets the FBI now wanted to know about MAX Enterprises.

Her testimony against her former boss, Max Whitney, and possibly others the FBI were unaware of at this point, might provide a way for her to atone for not revealing the information to law enforcement close to thirty years ago. There were other secrets, but those were none of their business. Or should she say *Kent's* business?

Freddie had left him in the dark the last time they saw each other. He hadn't known about the danger she faced. Maybe he could understand the threat Max posed against Kent's life back then, once she revealed all the facts in the near future. Her boss, Max, threatened harm to her policeman boyfriend if she blabbed any of the criminal activities Max participated in. Instead of telling Kent and his fellow officers about the situation, Freddie chose to flee Kent's love to ensure his safety.

She'd taken her boss's hush money and created a new persona, that of a world traveler who earned her master's degree in art while she enjoyed Europe. Her degree had eventually allowed her to cut ties with Max and quietly settle down in a remote corner of rural Virginia.

Freddie shook off any regrets. The ring on Kent's finger testified to marriage and family. Amber's FBI man mentioned that his boss had grandchildren. He'd obviously moved on and enjoyed the family they had once dreamed about.

Instead of daydreaming, Freddie tried to concentrate on the drawing she'd been working on the day before. She opened her computer and electronic sketch pad to begin toying with her latest picture book spread for a story the publisher had approved. Her efforts only destroyed the digital image on the tablet connected to her desktop computer. She hit undo and closed her eyes. Light steps entered the room, signaling Amber's approach. The young woman laid a comforting hand on one of Freddie's shoulders and sat down next to her.

"What is going on between you and their boss?" Amber asked.

"When I worked at your dad's office, the police officer I dated was Kent Russell. I left without saying goodbye. I thought I'd done the right thing since his life was under threat if I revealed Max's secrets."

Amber's eyes widened as her mouth formed an O. Freddie felt heat rising in her cheeks.

"Now he's the boss in charge of that group out there, so you can see how this situation is awkward for both of us." Freddie stared at the computer without really seeing the screen.

"Did you love him?" Amber squeezed Freddie's hands.

"More than anyone else in my life, but when all the trouble came to a head, your father threatened harm to Kent if I leaked what I knew to law enforcement. I loved him enough to let him go." Freddie clicked on the computer mouse and deleted a misshapen hand on one of the characters.

"What about now? I hear he is widowed. Do you still love him?"

A tear dripped from Miss Freddie's eye as she nodded. "It's too late for us. The look on his face a few moments ago didn't spell anything but dislike for me."

Amber pulled her close. "Only God knows the future. Maybe the boss will change his mind. I have to leave now with Graham. I'll be praying for you two."

Miss Freddie smiled. "You better watch yourself or you might fall for your own handsome lawman." She laughed when Amber shrugged and stood up to run a finger over a woven wall hanging from Central America featuring heart-shaped patterns.

Freddie's amusement dropped like a fifty-pound box of clay when Amber said her farewells and headed out the door. She began rehearsing in her mind what she would need to say to her students when and if she returned to her art classroom.

A few moments later she knew she no longer occupied the office alone. The faint scent of Kent's mossy aftershave filled the room. Without looking, she could picture his arms crossed and his brow creased. She heard him clear his throat and waited for his words.

~~~~~

Kent forced words through his lips. "Why, Winifred?" He paused.

She turned to face him. Silver threads wove their way through honey-toned hair he'd once adored. Her skin still looked soft.

"I'm sorry, but what I did was for your own good."

"Stop. I don't want an apology." He held up his hand. "Just tell me why you left MAX Enterprises and what you knew about their crimes, so I can solve this case.

Freddie shook her head. "At the beginning there was no separation between our breakup, and the start of Max's criminal activities. If you want the whole truth, you'll need to hear the whole story. You might as well call me Freddie since you know how much I dislike Winifred."

"I'm listening, Winifred." He watched her squirm. Her mouth gaped. She'd lost his respect when she left him years ago without a hint of what went wrong in their relationship. It had taken a couple of years before he found someone to trust with his love. Not long after Winifred left, his brother had passed away in a car wreck. Mutual loss had woven Kent into the lives of his sister-in-law and preteen nephew, giving him a family that didn't disappoint. After their wedding he'd officially adopted his nephew Lachlan as a son. His family had given him what Winifred had taken away. He glared at her as she started talking.

"When Max hired Victoria, the way the company did business changed. Victoria added several newcomers to the staff who worked close by her side. I felt uncomfortable when Max asked me to hack into another company's data, and I confronted him."

"Hold up a minute. I'm going to need to know the names of Victoria's allies." He pulled a pen and pad of paper from his shirt pocket. His younger workers preferred to take notes on their cell phones. He still chose pen and ink. When his ballpoint only scratched, he held it up in the air and shook it.

Winifred's eyebrows rose above her blue eyes. She pointed to a mug
~~~~~

filled with pens sitting on a nearby bookshelf. She could still read him like a well-worn manual. He tore his gaze away from her knowing look and focused on the line of children's books shelved behind the coffee cup full of writing utensils. Why did she have multiple copies of the Winnie Gee picture books his grandkids loved? Winifred. Freddie. Winnie. "Winifred Gwendolyn Grimsley, it seems you have more than one secret."

"I..."

Crash. The whole house shook. Glass shattered. Voices echoed from the front of the house accompanied by the sound of splintering wood.

Kent grabbed Freddie by the hand, pulling her toward the rear of the house. She pointed to the backdoor and they hurried outside as footsteps could be heard tromping into the house.

"Do you have a vehicle back here?" His hand tightened around her warm one. He was duty-bound to protect her, even though she'd broken his heart.

"No keys, but..." She tugged him toward an old shed.

Chapter Two

Hoping to find a motorcycle or a four-wheeler, Kent stared at an old lawnmower and an assortment of tools. "What?"

"Hush." Winifred's whispered command silenced him as she stepped to the back of the shed and lifted a portion of the wall. She crawled through the portal into a dark space behind the opening and waved for him to join her.

A chill shook Kent's body, followed by a wave of heat as he climbed through the opening. Stepping to the side, he watched her lower the panel into place, taking away all traces of their hiding place. His chest tightened. He forced deeper breaths into his lungs.

Darkness and damp air surrounded them. He heard something slip into place and hoped the swish represented a lock sealing them in from the outside world, even though his mind fought against the closure. Winifred's hand gripped his as she led them farther into black nothingness. Trusting her to lead the way felt wrong. Protection was his job. Their hiding from the enemy rubbed against his training as a lawman.

Moisture dripped onto his hair. Cool, humid air filled his lungs as he pushed each inhale and exhale through his system. The space became smaller. His head brushed against something hanging from above. Kent's heart pounded. Breathing became even more difficult as they trudged along an uphill path for what seemed like an eternity. Claustrophobia hadn't bothered him in years. He stopped moving and reached out a hand to feel the wall.

"I need a minute."

Winifred halted. She gasped and whispered close to his ear. "I'm so sorry. I forgot about your fear of small spaces."

The warmth of her whisper against his cheek sent another wave of panic all the way to Kent's heart. His hand lifted toward where he thought her cheek might be. Halfway there, he paused. She was a witness and possible suspect in the case his team worked. Now wasn't the time to remember past love. Darkness blessed the situation since she couldn't read the emotions crossing his face.

"Are we staying here for a while, or is there a quicker way out?"

"In another fifty yards we'll be back to the outside world." Her hushed voice warned him to keep his conversation quiet.

"How can you be so sure?" He fought to keep frustration from his voice, but knew he failed.

She guided his hand to a rope anchored to the tunnel's side. Small knots rubbed against his palm as he edged forward toward her. When he reached where she stopped, his fingers touched five larger knots. "I see, make that, I 'feel' like you've had this escape planned for an emergency." He inhaled as a small measure of relief spread through his veins.

"I never trusted Max or one of his cohorts not to come after me. I check it often. The cave comes out near an old cemetery north of here."

"Great, we can die there and save the caretaker's transportation costs." Kent heaved a short-lived breath and started pushing her to move forward. The sooner he saw daylight, the better.

"Ha-ha. I have a friend living near the cemetery. He can provide transportation." Her feet shuffled along in front of his.

Kent's head bumped a ceiling rock. "Ouch." Reality check. She might have moved on to another man. That was a good thing, or so he told himself. Maybe not so good for the guy who would soon be another victim of lost love when the truth came to light about Winifred Grimsley.

"You should bend down a little. The height of the passage decreases from this point on." Her quiet advice made him want to smack his palm against a wall, but that would hurt in this rocky place.

"Now you tell me." Kent rubbed fingers across his forehead. He'd have a bruise tomorrow, but thankfully no blood dripped from the point of impact.

"Sorry."

She didn't sound apologetic. If he wasn't mistaken, he heard a stifled giggle. He pushed around her and hunched over with one hand waving above his head, the other touching her guide rope. His feet shuffled forward, searching for objects that might obstruct their movement. The sooner he could catch a breath of fresh air, the better.

~~~~~

Freddie scrambled to keep up with Kent as he took the lead. She shouldn't have laughed at his injury, but she reacted without thinking due to the reality of the last hour's events finally settling in. She could only imagine the anger and panic in the usually calm man. His labored breathing echoed in the air around them. Thankfully the volume was quiet enough to let her listen for any followers or anyone ahead. He would need to calm his respiration down before they got much closer to the far entrance to her escape tunnel.

When she first discovered the place, she'd found the remnants of an old still. Those moonshine runners from long ago provided a place for today's dash to freedom, fleeing with a Fed instead of from one. She swallowed back another giggle, knowing the mirth would only upset Kent more. A hint of fresher air let her know they needed to slow down.
~~~~~

She reached forward and managed to latch onto a belt loop. "Take it easy. Catch your breath. We don't want to alert anyone in the cemetery."

The tension on her fingers in the loop slackened as he slowed. She released her hold. They both paused. Their breathing grew slower and deeper. A dim glow from the far opening seeped into the darkness, the proverbial end of the tunnel.

Kent turned to lead them once again. This time each slow step produced little sound. As they approached the outside light, she saw him remove a gun from inside his jacket and hold it in his left hand. For the first time in a long time Freddie felt protected. She didn't realize how much she'd missed the emotion as it wrapped around her like a warm blanket.

Swish. Something scurried ahead of them, jolting Freddie back to reality. Kent's forward movement paused as he lifted his weapon. She peered around his body. They both watched a fox skitter toward the light and disappear from view. Pent-up air flowed from Freddie's chest like a party balloon releasing its contents. Kent shook his head and resumed moving toward the light with slower steps. His even breathing brought relief to her mind. The claustrophobic attack had eased. She was sorry he endured it for her safety, but glad they made it through the tunnel unharmed.

Pop.

Pop.

Pop.

Freddie stiffened at the sound of a rifle. Kent pushed her against the tunnel wall and positioned himself in front with his gun poised.

"Get out of here, you nasty varmint." A deep voice, loud enough to wake sleeping souls, echoed across the cemetery.

Pop.

"I don't need you stealing any more chickens or their eggs."

~~~~~

Kent relaxed. Obviously, a farmer and the fox didn't get along.

Winifred laughed and poked her head under Kent's arm. "We're safe, once I let Rick know not to shoot at us."

Resisting the urge to wrap his arm around her shoulders as she slid out from behind, he stepped aside and lowered his weapon. Rick must be the friend she'd referred to earlier. A jealous streak slithered into his soul like a vicious snake. He needed to get out of the enclosed space and into the green meadow covered in headstones. Several crumbling monuments were visible through the foliage covering their exit.

"Let me look first to make sure he's the only one hunting out there." Kent made his way to the opening, gulping in the fresh air. He studied the area and waited.
~~~~~

Birds resumed tweeting. A breeze ruffled the plants hanging like a door to the outside world. He nodded for Winifred to step forward.

Instead of speaking, she whistled a tune. The melody resembled a bird's call without having the pattern of any species he'd heard before. Years ago, when he and Winifred dated, they'd bird-watched for a cheap outing. She probably enjoyed the activity with Rick now.

Kent heard footsteps coming closer until they stopped just out of sight.

The farmer laughed. "That sure sounded like a bird in distress. I hope that old fox isn't after you. Give me a few minutes while I take a gander down the road. If I don't see anyone coming, little birdie, I'll set you free to fly up to my old barn."

Rick's back appeared as he sauntered into the cemetery and inspected several headstone inscriptions. His bibbed overalls and straw hat covered his features as the man turned toward a gravel road edging the plots. His covered head moved from side to side before he wandered up the hill singing, "I'll Fly Away."

Winifred tapped his arm. "Follow me."

Fresh air provided plenty of energy as Kent jogged up the incline toward a ramshackle building. Winifred ducked in through a side door. He followed. Much to his relief, the end of the building, away from their escape path, stood open. No more confined space. A dust-covered vehicle sat near the opening, looking like it had seen better days. He wondered when someone last drove the beat-up means of transportation.

A shadow covered the man's face as he stepped into the building's open side. "Afternoon, Miss Freddie. Looks like you brought company with you."

"Rick, I'd like you to meet an old acquaintance of mine. This is Federal Agent Kent Russell."

Rick stepped into the musty barn and held out a gnarled hand. "I gather this isn't a social call. I hope you're here to defend my friend and not arrest her."

Kent returned the man's grip with a firm clasp, noting the white hair and wrinkled skin of the much older man. Rick appeared to only be a trusted friend, not a boyfriend to complicate the situation. "For now I'm protecting her as a witness. We're in need of transportation. Winifred mentioned you might be able to help."

The older man chuckled. "If you want to stay on this woman's good side, you better stick to calling her Miss Freddie. She doesn't favor her full name."

"I know." Kent fought against his lips curling upward as Winifred glared at him.

Rick's laughter flooded the building. "Interesting."

Winifred's arms crossed. "Enough. May we borrow Old Molly?"

Kent searched the space, hoping for a better mode of transportation.

"Are you looking for something, Mr. Agent?" Rick tapped the canvas top of the dusty vehicle, stirring up a small cloud. "This contraption is my Old Molly. I keep the jalopy tuned up for Miss Freddie and me to go mudding in the mountains when we need a break. Molly should provide you a good ride to wherever you need to go. Just get her back to me when you're done. I filled her tank the other day, so you have plenty to get you started."

Rick turned away and started walking from the building. "Come on up to the house. I'll get the keys and Miss Freddie can pack some snacks for wherever you're headed."

Kent had no choice except to follow the other two, who headed farther up the hill to a well-cared-for home. He took note of their surroundings and checked to make sure no one else arrived to threaten them. Miss Freddie, make that Winifred, needed to be more cautious, instead of running up hills without checking for danger. He paused. Climbing the steep terrain would take some getting used to. The flatlands surrounding his Ohio office didn't provide many mountains to scale.

After ascending a few more steps, the phone in his left pocket buzzed. Kent waited until he'd entered Rick's screened porch before checking his device. When he pulled the cell out, several texts had arrived, one after the other. The screen revealed multiple messages from the same unknown sender. The cemetery valley must be a dead zone for cell service. He'd have to watch for lack of reception as they traveled through the mountains.

Anger scorched through his chest when he read the first threatening message.

Chapter Three

Kent's personal phone's screen revealed a series of pictures featuring his grandchildren, Mason and Jordan. The same message accompanied each photo.

Give up the witness or your family will pay.

He studied the images as fire coursed through his veins. The pictures were recent, based on the mountainous background behind the two boys he loved. Almost a year ago his son Lachlan and daughter-in-law Chelsea, had moved away from Ohio to live in a major town in Virginia. The temptation to request a transfer to be near them had been strong. He had plenty of vacation time he rarely used, and they often came back to see him. The family had come for a visit recently to celebrate the youngest boy's birthday. One of the cell's photos pictured young Jordan holding the Winnie Gee picture book Kent had given him at that event. Some of his co-workers had come for the party, along with a former foster child, Melissa, and her adoptive parents. At least the messages had no reference to Melissa and her new family.

Pulling out his recently issued work cell from his right pocket, he sent a quick one-word message to his son. *Marvelous.* When Kent left police work to become an agent, he'd set up a code word with his family in case something bad went down. Lachlan would see the word sent from the anonymous number and know he needed to go into protective mode.

At least Kent had a new phone that Martin the mole had no control over. Not only had Martin managed to kidnap Max's young daughter, Jade, now he was threatening the Russell family children. Kent's ire grew. The enemy had made a big mistake. Protecting the witness might take on a secondary role to saving his family.

Ping

Another message appeared on his personal phone with an image of his former foster granddaughter, Melissa, pushing the Hallmarks' toddler in a stroller. Great. The enemy left no stone unturned. Kent typed a hasty reply.

You better watch your own back, Martin.

The next message appeared with an evil laugh emoji.

Martin and his boss lady are the least of your worries. They're nothing compared to me. Your witness owes me. Give her up and save your family.

Clue one. The texting person must be one of the other major players in this case. Kent wasn't going to sit around and play mouse to that cat's game. He needed to take an offensive stance and go now. He stormed into the house like a roaring lion and stomped over to the kitchen where Winifred and Rick were stuffing food into a backpack. Grabbing her shoulders, he twisted her around so he could look into her eyes.

"What are the names of the other people you suspected, besides Max, when you left MAX Enterprises?"

Winifred gasped and stepped out of his grasp. "You could ask in a nicer voice."

Rick pushed his way between the two. "I agree with the lady. A little honey goes a long way."

"I listened to her honey a long time ago, and it didn't get me what I wanted." Kent took a deep breath. "But you're right. I need to act rationally. Sit down. I need that information now." He pulled his paper pad from his pocket and waited.

Rick stood to the side with hands fisted on hips, looking ready to come to her defense.

Winifred flattened her hands on the table and glared at him. "There were several. Alexander, Victoria, and Marcus may have been in on the scheme, but I can't swear to any of them being involved. Max kept me out of the loop once I made my accusations. Why is there such a hurry to know this information right now?"

"I've become aware of a threat to my family. I need to know who I might be dealing with. There was a mole named Martin who helped kidnap Amber's younger sister, Jade, but it sounds like he may be working with a woman. I'm guessing that Victoria would probably be working with Martin. Tell me more about Alexander and Marcus. I want their full names so I can let the agency know."

Winifred leaned back in her chair with closed eyes. Her messy bun looked about to fall out of its clasps when she shook her head. "I can't remember much. Marcus Stanley spent half the day in Max's office several times a week. Alexander Johnson spent more time flirting with the younger women in the office than working."

Kent wondered if Winifred had flirted back. He bit back a retort as she continued. He needed all the ammunition he could gather.

"Then Max would issue a travel expense voucher and Alexander would disappear for a week or two. I was relieved when he left for his trips."

Good. "Do you have physical descriptions of these two men?"

"Alexander was a tall blonde who thought he was God's gift to the world. Back then, he wore a mustache. He liked taking advantage of his blue eyes to capture attention. Marcus was stockier and looked like he worked out. His hair and eyes were dark brown. He had a temper when things didn't go his way." She rubbed her arms.

"Did he ever threaten you?" Kent leaned closer. This sounded more like the type of man who would harm children to get his way.

"Let's just say that one of the conditions I put in my severance package was that Max would make sure Marcus never knew where to find me. Max kept that promise, as far as I can tell."

"Why were you afraid of him?"

A fleeting frown crossed her face before she continued.

"Alexander may have been an open flirt. Marcus had other ways of approaching women. He didn't give me much choice except to threaten him with a harassment charge. He pushed back with a countersuit after I slapped him when I worked late one day. It wasn't long afterward that I made my deal with Max."

"Do you think the man might be capable of harming children?" Kent flipped his pen between his fingers and then tapped on his notepad as he waited.

Winifred wrapped her arms around her middle and shivered. "I can't say for sure what the man would be capable of doing. When Amber visited, she often scooted under my desk and played when Marcus came through the office. He never said anything to her in my presence, but she seemed reluctant to be around him. Maybe she sensed my own fear. She wasn't a big fan of Alexander either." She paused and looked at Kent. "Has there been a threat to your grandchildren?"

"Yes. He sent pictures of Lachlan's boys and a former foster child." Kent's fist closed around his phone as he turned the device off. He slapped it down on Rick's table.

Salt and pepper shakers vibrated along with the anger and fear bubbling in his chest.

"I'm so sorry." Her forehead wrinkled. "I thought Lachlan was your nephew."

Winifred's quiet apology and question did little to soothe his anger. "It's too late for an apology. If you really want to know, after my brother died in a wreck, I married Lachlan's mother. We had a good life." His fingers tapped the pad of paper before continuing. The safety of Kent's family needed to be at the forefront of his thoughts.

"What I need now is some help. I should be placing you in a safe house. Instead, I'm going to ask if you're willing to wait for that security until I can set up a trap to capture this criminal before he harms my family. Are you willing to work with me?"

Before she could respond, Rick leaned in between them. "I don't like this. You can leave Miss Freddie with me. I'll make sure she's safe, even if we have to hide in the tunnel or up on the mountains."

~~~~~

Freddie held up a hand toward Rick and waved him away. "I can't let innocent children suffer because of my mistakes. I'll do what Kent asks. I've made bad choices in my life. The time has come to pay for the past."

Rick shook his head. "I don't like it, but you've always been a stubborn woman. If you change your mind, you know where to find me." He sank into a chair in apparent defeat.

She looked away from her faithful friend and faced her past. "What did you have in mind, Kent?"

"We're going to need a place to meet that will put us at an advantage over the man. He needs to be under the impression that I am going to hand you over to him in order to keep harm from my grandchildren. Marcus will be suspicious that I would even follow his directions, so the ruse has to come off as authentic."

"Maybe you could tell him I've agreed to give myself up of my own free will since I have a love of children. He would probably remember my relationship with Amber." Freddie closed her eyes and prayed she'd made the right choice to sacrifice herself. The blame for this whole situation sat squarely on her shoulders. If only she'd confessed to Kent years ago about what she suspected Max and his cohorts had done. She might have been the one with grandchildren who loved reading Winnie Gee's illustrated picture books and not living under a threat.

Kent's fingers drummed out a rhythm on the table. Freddie's eyes opened to his glaring face. He cleared his throat. "That would be too obvious. This guy wants to hunt us down. We've got to leave him a bread trail leading to an isolated place where we can take the scumbag down without harming a bunch of innocent bystanders. He's got to feel like he's in charge."

"Shouldn't you have some backup? I can help with that if you need me." Rick's familiar voice of reason reassured Freddie that she wasn't alone in this fight.

Kent nodded in agreement. "I'll be contacting our closest office, but it will take them a while to arrive from Roanoke. I'm not sure how much time we have before this guy latches on to the location of my phone coming alive with his texts. Max's acquaintances seem to have plenty of technology at their service."

"We could use that to our advantage. If Marcus is following your phone's location we can turn it back on once we're on the move. Send him
~~~~~

a message saying you'll need to think about turning me over to him." Needing a distraction, Freddie stood and retrieved the pack of food she and Rick had prepared. She hugged the bag close to her chest, hoping to hide her shaking body behind her backpack.

"We need to go somewhere that has hiding places. Do you know any locations that might work?" Kent stood and looked out the kitchen window.

Rick nodded. "There are two abandoned train tunnels underneath the stone face rock north of here. You could make it look like my old Molly jalopy didn't get very far and hide out in those."

Confidence filled Freddie's body as she straightened from leaning over the pack of food. "I've hiked those before. We'd be able to see him coming before he could spot us in the dark." Then her thoughts turned to what would possibly be a shooting situation. "What if Marcus brings his own backup?"

Rick laid his palm on the gun he'd placed on his countertop. "Then you might need me to ride shotgun until your official help arrives."

Kent's gaze moved from Rick to Freddie before nodding. "I'll use my business phone to let the office in Roanoke know about our plan. We'll meet somewhere in between here and there. Maybe they will know of a safe house we can use once we capture the person that we assume is Marcus. In the meantime, both of you need to follow my orders and not try anything without my consent. Do you understand?"

Freddie nodded and watched as Rick agreed and filled a belt with ammunition for his gun. They were all quiet as they headed for Molly's shed and climbed into the older vehicle. Rick sank into the driver's seat with Kent literally riding shotgun. She secured her seatbelt in the backseat and tucked the food onto the floor as Kent's phone came to life. His tapped message to the enemy echoed in the silence before they took off.

Molly rattled down Rick's gravel driveway, leaving a trail of dust behind. A few minutes after they headed north, the roar of a powerful vehicle drew closer.

Chapter Four

Kent checked the rearview mirror as a large pickup loomed nearer. If this was the enemy, they'd picked up his cell's signal too soon for him to set up any kind of ambush. He drew his handgun and prepared for the worst-case scenario. The flimsy windows and doors of Rick's jalopy wouldn't withstand an attack. When he looked at Winifred in the back seat, his heart sank. The crazy woman was waving to the occupants of the truck.

"Get down, Winifred. We don't need you drawing the attention of the criminals."

She laughed and pressed her palm down on the hand holding his weapon. The truck drew nearer and then passed them on a straight stretch of road. A male teen, with long bangs flapping in the breeze, leaned out of the window and yelled, "Hey, Miss Freddie. I miss your art classes."

She shook her finger at the kid and tapped her seatbelt. The kid grabbed for his seatbelt as the truck roared into the distance before turning off at a building labeled with high school signage.

He groaned. So much for anonymity. At least the perps hadn't caught up to them. "How much farther is it to this stone face?"

"We'll be there in about ten miles, but this road doesn't lend itself to high speeds between small burgs and curves." Rick took the next turn with enough speed to press Kent's shoulder against the side of their vehicle. Point taken.

Kent straightened in his seat, surveying both what was ahead and behind them as they passed tree-covered countryside and small-town businesses. Spring fragrances of blooming trees came and went. Once they headed north, the curves in that road became more frequent. A short time later, Rick slowed and drove old Molly to the side of the road. Gravel crunched under the wheels as the vehicle rolled to a stop.

"Here we are. Take a gander at our local wonder." Rick pointed up at jutting rocks.

Kent took in their surroundings as he climbed out of the car, stood, and closed his door. A creek gurgled nearby. Trees towered on either side of the road. High above, a large rock formation loomed with what resembled a person's visage. He spotted a short trail across the road leading up to a railroad track, looking like it circled around the edge of a bluff running parallel to the road.

Rick stepped to the front of his vehicle and lifted the hood. "I'll leave this up so Molly looks like she's had some engine trouble."

"Good, now let's get up that trail and find those tunnels you told me about." Kent grabbed Winifred's arm and pushed her behind him when a car came barreling around the curve.

Once the car passed, she shrugged out of his grasp and followed Rick across the road. He stomped along behind them, still checking for followers, relieved not to be touching her, but wishing he could. He pushed those ridiculous thoughts out of his mind and concentrated on watching his steps on the rough path up the hill. Once they reached the railroad tracks, he focused on placing his feet on the worn ties, half covered in loose gravel. A twisted ankle was the last thing he needed, but it did give him an idea as they made their way into the entrance of the first tunnel.

"Hey, Rick, how good are you with that rifle of yours?" Kent turned on his phone flashlight to illuminate the darkness. The shadowed area wrapped them in coolness. At least the space was big enough to not create any claustrophobic feelings. Now that he'd opened the phone for tracking, they needed to set up their trap as soon as possible.

"I can defend myself and Miss Freddie if you're asking." Rick's voice echoed off the side walls as they walked through the cavernous opening in the mountain. The volume of their steps increased as they tromped through the enclosed space.

"I'm not totally helpless, you two." Winifred's irritation came through loud and clear as light appeared from the exit to the tunnel.

"But what if it looked like you were helpless? That might work as a distraction when Marcus, or whoever is after us, follows us here." Kent swiped a spider web from his shoulder and rubbed his hands together before shaking the sticky mess off to one side as their steps crunched out of the cool tunnel. Sunshine warmed his face, temporarily impairing his vision, but not his thoughts. "Rick could hide near this tunnel and come behind them afterward. We'll go ahead and station ourselves outside the entrance to the next one. Winifred can be on the ground holding her ankle. I'll be in the next tunnel's shadows, ready to defend you while Rick comes from behind."

Winifred gave an unladylike snort. "I like the idea except for one thing. I don't want to be the melodramatic woman on the railroad tracks, waiting for the evil villain to come for me. How about Kent pretends to be the one injured? My role could be as the concerned nurse who comes to his rescue." She laughed. "That would also leave me free to run like crazy into the tunnel if you men start firing wild bullets."

Leave it to Winifred to complicate things. She'd certainly done her share of running in the past. Kent resisted the urge to slap his forehead and groan. He paused to give her idea some thought and realized it might work. He could roll to his stomach from a seated position and be ready to shoot from there if they needed to exchange fire. He hoped Marcus would realize his disadvantage when they confronted him from both directions and would give up without having to resort to guns or a more physical confrontation.

"Are you willing to give it a try, Rick?

"Anything for Miss Freddie, she's one sweet lady."

A sour taste filled Kent's mouth as he nodded. "Remember, we're looking for a short, stocky guy if he's alone. If he brings along backup, listen to their conversation as you follow at a distance. We don't want to harm any innocent victims."

Rick nodded and headed for a hiding place. He poked at the bushes with his rifle. Kent watched and realized the man was smart to check for snakes or other creatures before going into his camouflaged hideout.

Winifred rubbed her arms, looking concerned. "While we think it could be Marcus, there's always the possibility of Alexander or someone they've hired showing up. Before you two cowboys take any action, the smart thing would be for me to call out a name if I recognize anyone. That way you can be sure to take down the right person."

"That will work as long as one of our suspects shows up. We'll have to use our best judgment otherwise. Come on, Winifred. Let's go on ahead for our part of this setup." Kent headed out, listening to the tap of her footsteps as she followed him down the track. He sent a prayer heavenward. He didn't like using civilians in dangerous situations. They could use all the help they could get.

<div style="text-align:center">~~~~~</div>

Miss Freddie followed Kent, placing each step on the solid railroad ties while avoiding loose stones strewn across the way. The scent of his aftershave blended with the mossy earth. An occasional glimpse of Kent's broad shoulders brought memories of better days. She had loved him with all her heart back before Max forced her hand. He'd been with her when her life spun out of control during her mother's sudden death due to cancer and her father's reckless choices afterward.

When Kent arrested her dad on a drunken driving charge, he'd been the one to point her wayward parent toward a group that led to sobriety and a new outlook on life. Dad and his new wife were the only ones who knew where Freddie lived. They understood the need to keep her location quiet. Dad and Lindy were enjoying retirement out west, leaving past acquaintances behind for her sake, including Dad and Kent's once close relationship.

She stifled a sigh. Dad sometimes reminded her that he regretted not being able to contact the man who had saved him from himself. After this adventure was over, Dad might get his chance. Kent would hopefully offer more friendship to her parent than the treatment she received at the moment.

The second tunnel loomed ahead, darker than the first one. In her experience, most people only walked to the first passageway before turning back down the trail to their cars. Spider webs covered a portion of the entrance, sending a shiver down her spine. She was the one who agreed to run for cover if there was trouble.

Steady drips, coming from overhead, made the first few ties inside and outside of the space slippery. She looked to the side and spotted a fallen limb that might make a good weapon, if she decided not to retreat. She stepped over the metal rail and picked up the walking stick-sized limb. She stripped a few stems off, making it look even more useful. Sap covered her fingers with the scent of the forest.

"What are you doing?" Kent turned back to stare at her.

"I'm making you a support to lean on because of your fake injury." Not quite the real reason, but it still sounded like a valid excuse. She held her breath until he acknowledged her thought process with a jut of his clean-shaven chin. She headed for the tunnel and used the stick to sweep some of the webs from the entrance. At least there would be a clearer path if the option of running into the darkness became her only choice.

She watched Kent take his place on the tracks. He pulled his weapon from the holster, ran a routine that looked like he checked for ammunition and pulled the safety before setting it on the ground. Freddie lifted a prayer and took a stand next to him, leaning on her prop. Neither one spoke. Their attention focused on the empty track while they waited. As their movements slowed, the birds began to sing.

Her thoughts wandered again to happier times when they'd found time to admire feathered creatures and nature. They'd both enjoyed riding horses at a small riding stable. Kent had taught her everything he knew about horses, fulfilling a childhood wish. The owner had been a family friend of his, and they'd worked out a deal to earn riding time by helping clean stalls and animals. Bathing their mounts was fun, moving the stinking manure, not so much. Kent had covered for her while she did other chores that used her talents.

Freddie had painted signs for the business, using her artistic skills for something she and the company both loved. Making the signs had been more fun than cleaning duties. Her favorite horse, a gelding named Moose Face, had inspired one of the characters she used in several of her earliest picture books credited to Winnie Gee. Kent had always ridden a mare named Saucy.

She wondered if Kent ever got his chance to be on the mounted police force. She opened her mouth to ask but decided to clamp her lips shut instead. His frowning face hinted that he wasn't in the mood for a conversation. Warmth filled her as she endured his glare. She turned away and studied their surroundings.

A pair of squirrels chattered and bushes wavered as an unknown creature scuttled in the underbrush. Freddie breathed in the fresh air and studied the huge formations creating a cliff above their heads. Maybe they should have had Rick hide above them. She stretched her neck as she gazed at the ancient rock face hovering above. A few mountain laurels were budding, bringing spots of pink and purple to the hillside. Time seemed to slow as she stood next to Kent in awkward silence. Then the birds quieted. Gravel crunched under approaching footsteps. Freddie squeezed her hands tighter around her walking stick. Kent moved into his position, playing the role of an injured hiker as two men stepped into view. One of them was a stranger. The other...

"Alexander?"

"Hello, sweetheart. Were you expecting someone else?"

"I had Marcus pegged for being the one to come after me."

"Oh he's waiting for us to join him later today. I promised him I wouldn't take you out in the meantime. He has some questions for you. It looks like your watchdog is lying down on the job. I think he understood my messages and is ready to roll over and play dead if he hasn't really injured himself." Alexander sneered as he focused on Kent rubbing an ankle. "Either way, that takes out one complication."

The other man pulled out a weapon and waved it toward Freddie. "Move over here, woman."

"I don't think so." Freddie brandished her stick.

Kent rolled into firing position. "I'm a federal officer. You need to put down your weapon and surrender."

"Not happening, Fed." Alexander's companion pointed his gun at Kent.

Both men fired, sending spattering rocks into the air. Freddie screamed and ran into the fray with her stick poised like a lethal weapon.

Chapter Five

Kent shot blindly at Alexander's sidekick. The criminal had missed his mark but managed to spray Kent's eyes with debris. He felt more than saw Winifred brandishing her stick like a Ninja warrior as she rushed forward with a banshee scream. The *thunk* of metal hitting the ground rang in his ears. Scraping dust from his eyes, he watched Alexander flee from the scene as she repeatedly thwacked her stick across the body of the disarmed man. Kent spotted the fallen weapon, retrieved it, and again called for surrender.

"Call her off, and I'll give up. This isn't worth what that man paid me to do." The henchman raised his arms. "I was hired to scare you off so that coward could grab the teacher, not fight for my life." A stream of foul-smelling tobacco juice punctuated the man's words.

Kent jutted his chin to the side. Winifred stepped back but hovered nearby with her stick held ready to fight. He ordered the man to his knees and bound the criminal's hands behind his back.

"It was dangerous for you to get into the fight. Attacking him wasn't your smartest move." Kent shook his head. The woman was going to get them killed.

"You're welcome. I was glad to help disarm this guy." She crossed her arms while still grasping her stick. "For your information, there's more to teaching these days than just instruction. Surely you're aware that teacher training includes defending our students from harm. Even the children know of ways to use what they can for an attack in worst-case situations. I'd say this qualified."

Kent clamped his mouth shut as voices echoed from back down the tracks. He was aware of the required ALICE training. He'd just been surprised to see her in action. And maybe he'd felt shame for not being able to defend her. Make that defend the witness. After all, that was what she should be to him, a witness in a case.

Alexander came into view as he trudged down the tracks, with Rick pointing his shotgun at the man's back. The older man walked far enough behind the captured felon to avoid any confrontations.

"Looks like we caught our crooks," Rick bellowed. "I called the sheriff after I heard the gunshots. He should be here in a bit."

"Thanks, Rick. You did well." Winifred pounded the tip of her stick in the ground.

Alexander sneered. "You still have to worry about Marcus and his crew. This isn't over until we get what we want from you or take you down."

Kent blocked out the truth in the man's comment. "Get on your knees and put your hands behind your back."

Alexander complied. As Rick covered them with his shotgun, Kent bound the man's hands behind his back and read their Miranda rights. Helping both men to their feet, they began their trek back toward the parking area where they'd wait for the sheriff.

The henchman's mouth started working seconds later. "I'm sorry I got involved with this man. My name is John Haskins. Alexander hired me to come along with my gun to scare the lady. I shot near you. I didn't want to kill anyone."

"Shut up, John. I've got a good lawyer if you can keep your mouth shut. Otherwise, you're on your own." Alexander pushed his shoulder into John, making them both stumble as they walked between the rails.

Kent steadied John as Alexander tumbled to the ground, scattering gravel and scraping his cheek. "You can talk all you want, Mr. Haskins. Anything you give us will make your case lighter when we head to trial. Someone who will face sentencing for international crimes has used you. Choosing to side with him would not be wise."

Alexander interrupted their conversation with an overdramatic moan. "Can't you see I'm bleeding? I'll get off from whatever you charge me with because I'm claiming police brutality."

"I'm a federal agent, not the police. I think I can count on two or three other witnesses who saw you cause your own fall when you intimidated your accomplice to keep quiet. We'll be adding harassment of a potential witness to your cyber crimes and attempted kidnapping."

John frowned at the fallen man. "You can count on me as a witness. I'm not siding with Alexander anymore."

"Good for you." Winifred smiled at John. Kent turned away, not wanting to see her approving expression.

Except for the sound of their feet marching down the tracks, silence reigned until they reached the parking area. Kent separated the men by having Alexander sit near the woods beside the jalopy with Rick on guard duty. John sat, leaning against a newer model SUV parked behind old Molly. His mouth worked as he chewed the remnants of his wad of tobacco.

Kent squatted next to John. The man's foul breath, laced with a hint of alcohol, tainted the air, but getting answers was more important than reacting to the stench. "Did he tell you much about his partner Marcus?"

"Only that he was heading north to check on someone's grandkids. That sounded strange to me. Like I said, I just needed to get a few dollars and then bug out." Tobacco juice leaked from the side of John's mouth.

Kent slammed his hand on the side of the SUV, adding to the pain filtering through his body and soul. He stood and walked away. Fighting the urge to take his anger out on both men, he rubbed his aching hand as he paced. The need to get to his grandchildren before Marcus did overcame any desire to complicate the situation further. Winifred's description of the man's personality did not bode well for their safety.

In the distance, sirens echoed through the wooded area. It was about time the locals showed up. He'd turn their captives over to the sheriff and commandeer Alexander's car as federal evidence. Using the excuse to frisk Alexander, he located the SUV keys and pocketed them.

Alexander laughed. "Taking my car isn't going to help you, Mr. Fed. I'll add stealing to my lawyer's countersuit."

~~~~~

Freddie walked a few steps to the edge of the nearby creek. Seeing the rippling water soothed her shattered nerves. Taking a stand against the enemy had shaken her. Hitting someone wasn't in her nature. She stared upward through the trees.

Lord, forgive me for taking things into my own hands. I sure don't feel good right now about harming another human. Help me to trust You and do the right thing in the future.

As she studied the world around her, the sun warmed her face and a family of chattering chipmunks played on a rock, making her smile.

Maybe Kent had a right to be mad at her. She shook her head. He certainly had no reason to trust her after she'd dumped him years ago. Freddie threw her walking stick into the creek and watched it work its way downstream. The past was the past. She needed to survive this ordeal so Kent could solve this case and they could move on. Her faith was important. She would need every ounce of her belief if she ended up serving time for not reporting the crimes at MAX Enterprises years ago.

Her past choices were leaving her students without their familiar teacher. She was one of the few traveling teachers who had lasted more than a year or two in the rural situation. Several music and physical educators had come and gone during Freddie's tenure. Last year's music teacher had given notice and moved to another district halfway through the year. The latest physical education instructor mentioned he'd be moving after May to a coaching position in a larger school system.

Freddie's work, as Winnie Gee the illustrator, would probably fade into oblivion once her agent heard about her involvement with a crime. At least that part of her life remained mostly anonymous. Amber was one of the few who knew about Freddie's second career as an illustrator. The young woman's knowledge had only been shared hours ago. So far, Kent hadn't fully discovered that part of her life due to the recent interruption
~~~~~

and chase. Though, if his unanswered question meant anything, he probably wondered about her illustrations left open on her computer. There'd been no time to close them down. She usually tried to back up her files to the cloud but couldn't be sure the latest were saved. What if the intruders had destroyed her work for the next book? Would it matter when life as she knew it ended?

Whoop, whoop.

The sheriff blasted his siren as he pulled away. Freddie jumped. Taking one last look at the creek, she headed back to where Rick and Kent leaned against the two vehicles.

Rick stepped forward and wrapped his arms around her. "Take care of yourself, Miss Freddie. I'm looking forward to catching up with you when all this is said and done."

She managed to hold her reaction to a couple of sniffles and a tight squeeze for the man who represented the closest thing to having a parent, while living her obscure life as a county teacher. "I'll do my best to come back, my friend."

Kent shook Rick's hand. "Thanks for the help. We need to get going, Winifred. My grandchildren's lives are on the line." He turned and headed for the criminal's SUV, stopping by the passenger door. He held it open and waited.

Freddie was tempted to smile at his courtesy. Instead, she hurried to take her place in the front seat of the vehicle and buckled up as he closed the door. Guilt filled her over the threats to his grandchildren. Once he had settled into his seat and started driving down the road, she sneaked a peek at his profile. Though he looked to be deep in thought, the earlier anger didn't linger.

"I'm sorry." Their voices rang in harmony. She opened her mouth to speak.

Kent lifted one hand from the wheel. "I accept whatever apology you were going to offer. Losing my temper back there was not acceptable. I appreciate the help you gave. I don't know if I could have taken the man down without your assistance. As an agent, I need to be more professional about this whole thing, even if it does involve people that I love." His cheeks took on a ruddy hue.

Warmth filtered up Freddie's neck as he returned his hand to the wheel. Did he mean he still had feelings for her, or was he only referring to his grandchildren? She took a deep breath, trying to clear her thoughts.

"Are we heading to your grandchildren's home to make sure they are safe?"

"The first stop is to drop this car at our regional office in Roanoke so they can inspect it as evidence. That's the proper procedure, and what I promised the local sheriff back at the old stone face. I'll recruit someone to take you to a place where you will be safe from harm. Then I'll partner up with another agent to help ensure the safety of my family."

The GPS voice interrupted their conversation, directing them north and out of the mountains.

Freddie nodded. She wasn't part of the family he wanted to protect. An aching sense of loss sank into her chest. She'd given Kent up years ago. Deep down, she realized she'd been hoping for a reconnection that wasn't going to happen. Turning her gaze forward, she watched the scenery flash by as curvy mountain roads led to foothills, and two lanes gave way to four-lane roads and highways. When the GPS voice rang in her ear with the command to "keep right," Freddie wished she'd made the right choice long ago. As light faded to darkness, her eyes closed. Restless memories of working for MAX Enterprises and dating her handsome policeman fought to rule her dreams.

"Wake up, Winifred. Something's wrong with this vehicle."

Kent's voice startled her from her storm-tossed dreams. The SUV swayed from side-to-side as her head banged against the passenger window.

"What are you doing?"

"The problem is, I'm not doing anything. Someone has taken over the computer on this car. Try not to tighten your body on impact." He grabbed her hand. They headed straight for a guardrail.

Freddie tried to relax but couldn't stop screaming as she jerked forward. The airbags exploded. Her chest ached. Her vision spun.

Chapter Six

Kent coughed as a cloud of airbag dust enveloped his face. His chest heaved. There would be a huge bruise from the impact, but at least he was conscious and alive. A moan sounded from the passenger seat. It sounded like Freddie had also survived.

"That was awful. Ouch. Do we need to get out of this car before it explodes or takes us on another joy ride?" She waved a hand at the settling dust. Then she reached for the handle and tried to open the door. It didn't budge.

He tried the one on his side with the same results. Whoever controlled the vehicle didn't want them getting out. After releasing the seatbelt, he fisted the metal end and began pounding it against the window. At first, nothing happened. He looked over and saw Freddie chipping away at her side with a can opener. Where she'd found that, he had no idea, unless it was part of Rick's backpack of food.

Finally, a tiny web of broken glass appeared in his window. Freddie leaned over him and used her tool to help widen the damage, until the window bent outwards. Using the backpack filled with foodstuff, they pushed until the window fell away.

Kent crawled up and out. He reached to steady Winifred as she shimmied out behind him, can opener scraping across the roof of the car. Placing his hands under her armpits, he lifted her free. Together, they headed into the brush at the side of the highway. Darkness gave them cover as they fled from the vehicle. Grabbing her hand seemed like the logical thing to do, even though it sent memories of better times bouncing through his brain. He dismissed those errant thoughts. His brain still roiled from the crash and their narrow escape. That was all.

Someone would come looking for them. Staying near the car would be one option to discover and capture Marcus or his henchmen. If they used hired henchmen, they might easily capture Winifred, since Kent was still dazed from the wreck. It might be a better option to hide far away from the wreck. He led them deeper into the weeds and small trees until they reached a fence that ran near the highway.

"How are you at climbing fences, Freddie?"

"I've gone over a few long ago." Her whispered answer warmed his ear as she leaned closer. She must have heard his use of her first name and decided to take advantage of his moment of weakness. Come to think of it, he may have thought of her as Freddie several times in the last few hours. He was slipping. Now wasn't the time to argue. He tossed the food pack over the fence and leaned against the barrier with his knees bent and braced.

Holding out his clasped hands, he boosted her over the top of the fence. Thankfully, there was no ribbon wire. He reached for the top rail and managed to follow her without looking inept. Not bad for an agent who had been seated at a desk for the last few years. Moonlight lit the field of six-inch-high corn in front of them. Too bad it wasn't fall when tall stalks would provide cover. A line of trees at the far end of the field would do.

"That way." He shouldered the backpack of supplies and once again took Freddie's, make that Winifred's hand. Hands clasped, they high-stepped through the young corn, making their way toward the tree line. "If we head to the other side of this field, we'll be more likely to find a road to walk or a farm building to hide in until we see daylight."

Winifred stumbled against him when he slowed near the trees. "I'm sorry."

"Now's not the time. We need to keep moving." Kent pulled on her hand.

"I wasn't apologizing for stumbling, I meant about causing this whole situation. If only I'd told you in the first place. I loved you too much to let Max harm you."

This time Kent was the one who stumbled. He should have been watching for the roots sticking out into the field instead of listening to her words. The temptation to say something about her love not being strong enough to trust his police abilities burned in his throat. Instead, he chose silence as he led them faster along the path he'd chosen.

He heard a slight huff from behind as he let go of her hand and marched forward. He focused on the life he'd had. His late wife and their cherished family were all that mattered. If it wasn't for Winifred, they wouldn't be in peril. Taking a moment to calm down, he breathed in the night air and looked up to the heavens peeping between the tree leaves.

"We can't relive the past. Let's get you and my family safe. After that you can go back to teaching here in Virginia, and I'll go back to my desk in Ohio."

"Fine. I need something to drink. Give me a minute to catch my breath." She held out her hand for the supply pack. She pulled out a water bottle and gulped down half.

He grabbed his own bottle and slaked his thirst. She had made the sensible choice. Why was she making him feel so angry? He should be the calm one. Normally that was the case. He bowed his head in prayer, seeking answers. The thoughts that came to mind were not ones he wanted to hear. Though he'd loved his wife with all his heart, it seemed he still fought against wanting to love Winifred with the affection of their past romance. Being cross wasn't going to solve the case, help his family, or give him peace.

"I'm sorry, too, Winifred."

Kent's phone rumbled in his pocket. Lifting it out, he found a message from his contact at the Roanoke branch, wondering when they expected to arrive. He sent back a text, explaining their approximate location. His contact conveyed a number for him to call when they reached an identifiable site. In the meantime, they'd track Kent's phone so they could get in the vicinity.

Kent reached for Freddie's hand and gave it a squeeze. They headed across the dark field toward an unknown future.

~~~~~

The spring night chilled Freddie, making her thankful for Kent's warm touch. She'd missed holding his hand, due to her own choices years ago. Maybe his clasp indicated forgiveness. She stumbled and his fingers tightened around hers.

Or maybe he only needed to keep her from falling in the unfamiliar territory. Mounded rows of dirt in the field and the forest's raised roots provided plenty of challenges to their walk. The smell of moist soil tickled her nose as their feet thumped against the ground. A crescent moon barely lit the darkness as they forged ahead. Dampness began to saturate her clothing, making her shiver.

"I hope we find a place to stop soon. I don't know if I'm shook up from the wreck or the cold, but my body is starting to shake." Freddie paused and wrapped her arms across her belly, trying to figure out what she needed.

"Did you and Rick put a jacket or blanket in the backpack?" Kent lifted the bag from his shoulders and placed it on the ground.

Freddie nodded, and then realized he probably couldn't see her from his bent over position. "We keep a picnic blanket in one of the side pockets. It's pretty ragged, but works to cover enough dirt for a wilderness meal."

She peered at his muscular silhouette as he reached into the pack and pulled the threadbare cloth out. He unfurled it over her shoulders, providing a little warmth. Her teeth still chattered.

"I'm going to hold you close to warm you up a little. Try to breathe deeply and don't dwell on what we've been through. I don't need you to go into..." Kent paused.

She had a pretty good guess about what he'd almost said. Shock could be dangerous if that was what was going on.

"I think it really is the cold. Maybe partly a reaction to what is going on, but I don't think I'm going into shock."
~~~~~

His arms closed around her, drawing her close to his chest. Warmth from his closeness and her overactive imagination sent flutters through her body. Breathing in his mossy aftershave reminded her of the love they'd once shared. The shaking subsided as Freddie began to relax.

She lifted her head for a moment. Kent stared off into the distance. A glint of light reflected off moisture near his eyes. She looked away. Pulling the blanket closer around herself, she backed out of his arms.

"Thank you. That helped. We can start walking again." She felt like running. She wanted to run away from the past, the rocky future they faced, and what was happening at the moment.

"No problem. I always take care of witnesses in my protection." His voice was stiff.

His dry comment reminded her to focus on their trek toward safety. Following that course was the best plan, even though disappointment threatened to bring back her earlier chill. She huffed out another deep breath and resumed their trek down the edge of the tree line. This time she avoided his extended hand and stepped into the lead. By concentrating, she discovered a pattern to the rows of raised soil at the edge of the cornfield. A dog barked in the distance, possibly a sign of a home located on a road where they could connect with the Virginia federal agents. Freddie told herself that she'd be glad when she wasn't bumping elbows with Kent all the time. Her heart told her something else.

Distant voices echoed across the field and interrupted her thoughts. Kent tapped her shoulder and motioned her into the wooded area. They made their way through several feet of undergrowth. Brambles snagged at the blanket, pulling it off her shoulders. She snatched her cover back and rolled it up into her arms as they stopped to lean against the rough bark of a pine.

Pollen made Freddie's nose twitch. Stifling a sneeze, she pushed the blanket against her nose to muffle the sound. Kent's squeeze to her shoulder seemed to urge caution. She only hoped she could control her allergic reaction until they were safe. Rubbing her nose helped some. She sniffed. Her shoulder suffered as Kent's clasp tightened. She pushed his hand away and peered around the tree.

A beam of light illuminated a path across the young corn crop. It seemed to originate from where they'd crossed the fence. Light swept the field from one side to the other, causing dancing shadows near each cornstalk. Freddie froze, not daring to move. Would Kent want to face the enemy again, or would they seek an escape? If it were her making the decision, it would be to run fast to someplace far away.

They knew Marcus was behind what had happened to them. Unless Marcus was out there in the field, wouldn't it be wiser to avoid his hired men and get to a safe place? The muffled voices from across the field sounded higher pitched than what she remembered Marcus sounding like.

"Do you think either of them could be Marcus?" Kent's whispered question resonated with her thoughts.

She shook her head. His warm breath tickling her ear tied her tongue in a knot.

He pointed to the opposite side of the tree line where another field grew. Moving out of the trees, they continued their journey away from the highway. Freddie's breath came quicker as they hurried toward the far end of the field. Holding hands became a necessity to protect either of them from falling in the increased darkness.

Deep shadows covered their path on the western side of the tree line, making it harder to see. A few clouds moved to cover the sliver of moonlight. In the distance a faint glow appeared from the shadowed outline of a farmhouse. Would they find a friend or a foe in the distant home?

Chapter Seven

Kent led Freddie back toward the cover of the trees and slowed their pace. The house looked inviting, but who knew what kind of reception they might receive this late at night? Most people wouldn't welcome strangers into their homes so late in the evening. Plus, he didn't want to put the homeowners in danger if the people back at the road were following them. He halted their movement. Leaning closer he whispered into her ear, trying to ignore the wisps of hair that brushed his cheek.

"I'm going to check the other field and make sure we don't have any followers." A sense of loss filled him when she dropped his hand.

He was in trouble in more ways than one. He reminded himself that Winifred was a witness. That was all. He didn't need to get emotionally involved, especially with the safety of his grandkids at stake. Personally taking on her case was a mistake, a conflict of interest. He should have traveled south with Max's daughter, Amber, and let another agent escort Winifred to a safe house.

His shoes crunched on something. He paused. Waited. Condemned himself for not concentrating. When he heard nothing else, he continued his cautious steps through the woods. Scanning the other field while standing in the shadowed trees provided no hint of anyone following. The situation looked good, but he decided to give it a few more minutes.

An owl hooted and received an answering call. Crickets chirped. Light came and went as clouds obscured the crescent moon and then hurried across the sky. His arms chilled as a breeze brushed his skin. A faint hint of lavender scented the air. She'd followed him through the trees. He hadn't heard her approaching, but he remembered her favorite perfume.

"Did you spot any trouble?" Her breath warmed his cheeks, or was that an unwanted reaction he wanted to tame?

"No. I think we're safe to walk on this side of the trees for now." He headed toward the house without holding Winifred's hand. The land was easier to see, so they no longer needed that connection. At least, that was his reasoning.

Kent turned his focus to the farmhouse. Curtains hid the people living inside, but several rooms were still illuminated. Car doors closing and laughter echoed from the far side of the house. The occupants must have been waiting for the late arrivals. Maybe their good mood would provide an easier introduction to the people inside. He prayed that might be the case. *Watch over us, Lord.*

Caution washed over his soul. Was God trying to tell him something? God and his gut seemed to have a pretty strong relationship when it came to thinking things through. He needed to check out the situation before they introduced themselves in the middle of the night.

Winifred stepped around Kent and marched toward the house as he contemplated their next step. He rushed forward and grabbed her arm. "Hold on a minute. I want to assess the situation before we barge in."

Her teeth chattered near his ear. "I hope you can make your decision soon. I'm freezing under this excuse for a blanket and since you don't have a coat, I figure you're cold too. The people talking a few minutes ago sounded like they were happy to be here. We should catch them before they call it a night."

"I want to be cautious. Something is bothering me about the situation, and I can't put my finger on..."

A back porch light shone in his eyes. His heart sunk in his chest. There would be no time to scope out the place.

A woman's trembling voice called out from the house. "Who's there? Identify yourself, or I'll be calling the sheriff."

"It's all right, ma'am. I'm a federal agent. We don't mean any harm. I only need your street address so we can call for someone to come pick us up. Help shouldn't be too far away since other agents have been tracking the general location of my phone."

He pulled Winifred closer, speaking under his breath. "Don't volunteer any information about yourself. I'll inform them if they need to know anything."

A woman wearing jeans and a dark sweater stepped out onto the porch. In the shadows, a man wearing a baseball cap stood behind her, saying something close to her ear. She waved them toward the house. "We want to see your identification and that phone for proof that you're telling the truth." A tremor shook her voice. "Tell that lady with you to bring the things to us."

Kent noticed an almost imperceptible shake of the woman's head. Was it a nervous tic or was she trying to warn him? The hidden man stepped away from the doorway, holding a shotgun to his shoulder.

Kent raised his phone and wallet in the air. "I'm telling you the truth, but here's your proof if you need it." With arms held high, he placed the items in Freddie's outstretched hands. "Be ready to run." He muttered for her hearing only. Her eyes met his and she nodded.

He watched as Winifred carried his phone and identification to the couple. The man inspected the two pieces and then waved the women into the house.

Shadowed figures rushed from behind him and from the sides of the house. Fists flew. Strong arms wrapped around him.

As he struggled to escape, the man on the porch sneered. "Come on in, Agent Russell. We've been expecting you."

~~~~~

When Freddie entered the house, someone gripped her middle and pulled her to the side. Kent's phone and wallet flew from her hands. Her captor kicked them to the side. She stomped on one of the man's feet. His arms tightened as he lifted her off the ground. Another man wrapped duct tape around her ankles, and then the first slammed her into a chair. He held her in place until they secured her hands to the seat.

The female who had lured her into the house whimpered as they put her in another chair. "I'm sorry, ma'am. They have my husband in another room. They threatened to..."

One of the men halted the sentence by gagging her. "Enough of your talk, lady. We'll be done with you soon enough."

The woman's eyes widened. Fear crawled down Freddie's spine. They would be lucky if either of them lived much longer. Thumping from outside brought her thoughts back to Kent. Maybe he would escape.

Her hopes faded when two dark-haired men dragged a battered Kent into the room. Zip ties held his wrists together as they taped him to another chair. He slumped forward as they frisked him and took his sidearm. She wondered if he'd passed out. If he was going to be in any shape to help them, she needed to stall for time. Maybe pretending to take a nap herself would give her time to think.

When she jerked awake later, she gazed around the room. Some of the men dozed while others stood guard. The microwave's clock indicated several hours had passed. She needed to come up with a plan sooner, rather than later. A box of toys and a few children's books caught her attention and her thoughts.

Freddie faced the gray-haired woman. "Are those for your grandchildren?"

A brief nod told her what she needed to know. "Do they come here often?"

The woman bobbed her head. Panic washed across her expression.

Freddie turned her focus on the men occupying the room. A dirty-blond hulk looked out windows while the two men who'd captured Kent snored as they leaned against a paneled wall. A fellow with an unkempt man-bun sat staring at a machine. The older guy with the gun still kept guard at the door. She studied their faces as she tried to figure out their motivation. None appeared well-dressed. Shaggy hair covered most of their heads. Rancid body odor emanated from their worn clothing. Their language spoke of hired men rather than cyber criminals.
~~~~~

Gray streaks threaded the gunman's beard. Freddie drew on her best teaching expressions and looked toward the older man with as much compassion as she could muster.

"Do you have grandkids, mister?"

He stared at her. She looked right back. His eye twitched.

"I have a feeling if we wait much longer this woman's grandkids are going to come barreling into this house, expecting to play with those toys over there. Are you going to threaten children and tie them up too?"

Graybeard looked away. Good. She'd put a chink in his armor. Now to prod a little deeper. "How much is Marcus paying you to keep us here? I have a few resources that might make a better deal for you."

One of the younger men laughed as he woke from his nap. "Don't know the boss man's name, but our pay is more than you can afford, lady."

Freddie lifted her eyebrows. "You never know. I've known Marcus a long time, and if he lets you live long enough to collect your pay, it will surprise me."

"You're just playing us. He's already paid us half. We just got to cash the money order. We're waiting for him to arrive. Once he gets here, we'll get the rest of our pay and he'll take you off of our hands. We don't know or even care what this guy's name is." The other former sleeper leaned forward in his chair.

Freddie forced a sad grimace onto her face. "Well, you know his name now and just like me, you will be on his list of witnesses to eliminate."

The captors looked at each other.

Hulk crossed his arms and frowned. "I don't know about the rest of the guys, but I'm hanging around for our man to show up with the money."

"What if the federal agents show up first? You heard Agent Russell mention he'd been in contact with them." Freddie glared back at the large man.

Graybeard laughed. "Our boss took care of that little problem. He taught Saul over there how to run a machine that jammed your phones once you two got out of the car."

Saul grinned. "Yup. That reply your agent sent to his people in Roanoke went right to me. I gave Agent Russell my cell number in case you got lost between here and the road." He placed his hand on a breadbox-sized metal container and gave it a pat.

A sense of doom washed over her. Freddie's vision narrowed for a moment as stars flickered in her peripheral vision. A flash of heat rushed to her chest. This wasn't the time for her to go into one of her rare panic attacks. She closed her eyes and took a deep breath. *Help me to say and do the right things, Lord.* Opening her eyes she focused on a framed reproduction of an old man praying over a meal. Her grandmother used to have one of those pictures hanging over her breakfast nook. *Thank You, Lord, for the opportunity to pray.* At least they hadn't gagged her like they'd done to the other woman.

She concentrated on the picture. A sliver of dawn's early sunlight brightened the illumination streaming into the scene. A Bible, glasses, soup, and bread ready to be sliced sat before a flannel-clad man bowed in prayer. The gray-bearded fellow reminded her of the one person who'd reacted to her concerns about the children.

Freddie turned her head and stared. He checked his watch as he leaned on his rifle and looked out the door's window. He finally returned her glance, after looking at the time again.

"If you live through Marcus paying you off, do you really want to be part of the murder of innocent children and their grandparents? Let these people go or allow them to call and cancel the grandchildren's visit. Marcus only wants me." She hated begging, but hoped somehow they'd allow the homeowners a chance to send a message to their family, signaling a problem.

The man turned away. "The boss should be here soon. I doubt any kids will arrive this early in the morning. I need that money for my own kin."

Freddie shook her head. One of Kent's fingers circled. He was awake. Was he trying to tell her to keep going? She looked back at the framed print on the wall. "Could you at least find some bread for us to eat? I'm starved." A brief frown wrinkled Kent's brow and then disappeared.

Graybeard left his weapon by the door and made his way to a loaf of bread sitting on the counter. He pulled a slice of whole wheat from the wrapped package.

Kent groaned loudly, shrugging his shoulders like an ancient dog.

What a ham. The thought of a honey-crusted ham made Freddie's mouth water.

"Oh man, do I smell food? You wouldn't happen to have some ham and cheese to go along with the bread?" Kent added another overdone groan.

Could the man read her mind? No doubt he was thinking of the past. They'd both enjoyed specialty ham sandwiches at a local joint when they'd dated. Ham It Up had been a favorite place to grab some quick food. Maybe he wanted her act to be a little emotive.

"You're breaking my heart, Kent, but how are we going to feed ourselves with our hands tied?"

Kent looked at the man holding the bread. Big eyes graced his face. "Maybe they could free our hands so we can eat."

"I'm not buying into that trick, agent." Hulk's voice echoed across the room.

Kent's eyebrows rose as he shifted his head to the side. He still slouched over in his chair. Was he hurt or hiding something from the crew of captors? "How about freeing Winifred? She won't be able to do much harm. I've heard she's pretty artistic when it comes to slapping a sandwich together."

"Then she can fix ours first." One of the younger men released Freddie's hands while Graybeard rummaged through the refrigerator and pulled out cold cuts, cheese, and mayonnaise.

Freddie shook out her wrists, glad to have them free. As they worked on freeing her feet, a moan came from another room. Saul left his command station next to the jamming device and headed out of the room. He returned with a staggering older man who had a goose egg-sized injury on his forehead. His eyes met those of the other captive woman. His shoulders sagged as they pushed him into Freddie's former seat.

"What are you waiting for? Start fixing those sandwiches."

"I could use a knife to spread the mayo."

Graybeard pulled open a couple of drawers and handed her a spoon. The spoon wouldn't offer much protection, but she'd take what she could get. Freddie stood at the counter. Quiet settled over the room. The jammer next to her hummed and then a loud ticking started. She backed away.

"Was this thing ticking before?"

Saul's eyes grew wide. "No."

Chapter Eight

Kent straightened and tossed aside the zip ties he'd managed to wiggle out of while pretending to sleep in a slumped position. The ticking probably indicated a bomb's timer counting down.

"Everyone needs to get out now. Take a captive with you. You'll be facing murder charges if you don't help us escape."

Graybeard was the first to react. He grabbed the female homeowner and dragged her seat out the door. A hulking man picked up the woman's husband, still tied to a chair, and carried him away. The other men scrambled out and ran. *Cowards.* Kent bent over and began working to free his legs from the chair. Freddie fell to her knees next to him, sawing away with a knife she must have found in a kitchen drawer.

"Save yourself, Freddie."

"No."

The stubborn woman broke through the tape on his right leg at about the same time he ripped through the left bindings. Running for the door, they grabbed hands and leapt from the porch. A roar pierced the air. A hot wind rushed from the house, pushing them toward the ground. Sulfur-tainted oxygen filtered into his nose and lungs. As they fell, he wrapped his body around hers and prayed for their protection. Warmth coursed across his back, but it didn't seem to burn for now.

"Come on, Freddie, we need to get further back." He scrambled to his feet and pulled her away from the burning home. He spotted the homeowners, still in their chairs, leaning against an older building. "Let's get them free. Maybe a neighbor will call in the inferno."

After freeing the homeowners, J.P. and Sarah Patterson, Kent asked where the kidnappers were.

"They dumped us and then took off in a black truck, leaving us nothing. My home is gone forever." Tears rolled down Sarah's face.

"At least we're alive." J.P. leaned on his wife and stumbled as they walked away from the flaming house.

"I don't suppose either of you have a phone on you so we can call for help?" Kent stepped closer to the older couple, attempting to hear their answer over the snapping and popping roar coming from the house. It didn't help that his ears were still ringing from the initial blast.

"We got a landline down in the barn you can use. There's a little office on the right side as you go in." J.P.'s answer gave Kent a glimmer of hope.

He hurried ahead of the others. Locating the phone, he called 9-1-1 and let them know about the fire at the Patterson home. The couple had registered the barn phone with emergency services and help was on its way. Kent also informed the operator that a black truck loaded with rough-looking men had left the arson and kidnapping scene. When fire trucks arrived and began working to settle the flames, he called his office.

"Hey, Dianne, it's Kent calling you from a borrowed phone. I need you to contact the Roanoke office and ask them to send a couple agents and an extra car to this address." He spelled out the location to his office assistant and let her know about the latest events. "Ask them to bring a burner phone. My phones aren't viable anymore. I need a safe house for Winifred Grimsley. We need a place that's well-hidden. I've identified another cybercriminal as Marcus Stanley. I'm pretty sure he was the one who hired the men to capture us last night. He was working with Alexander Johnson until we turned that crook over to the Lee County, Virginia sheriff."

"Uh, Boss. You should know Johnson got away from the sheriff. Somehow he made the car door locks open when the sheriff stopped to clear debris off the road. Another car pulled up and off they went, leaving the sheriff locked out of his patrol car. Alexander left the other prisoner handcuffed in the back seat. I tried to call you yesterday after it happened, but you didn't answer."

"Thanks to our cybercriminals I've been having issues with phones during this whole trip. Have you heard anything from Agent Graham and his journey with Amber Whitney?"

Dianne laughed. "You aren't the only one having trouble with your phones. Social media is causing all kinds of problems for Graham and Amber. The last I heard, they were traveling through Tennessee and headed for Georgia to collect more clues. Someone has definitely found a way to track them."

"Too bad they tracked them right to our key witness, Freddie." Kent looked out the barn door and couldn't see her anywhere. His heart rate sped up. She hadn't said much since their tumble to the ground.

"Freddie?" Dianne's voice hummed with curiosity. "Is there something I need to know, boss?"

The woman didn't need to know his history with their witness. Someone above Dianne's status would be calling for a conflict of interest and that was the last thing he needed. He avoided her question by moving on to his next concern.

"My grandchildren's lives are under threat. My son is hiding with his family, but I had a text mentioning a foster child they once cared for. Her name is Melissa. Scott and Ginny Hallmark from Forest Glen adopted her. I need you to arrange for the girl's protection."

"I'll get someone down there right away. Now why are you calling your witness by a nickname?"

The secretary was tenacious. She would make a good interrogator as long as he wasn't the one questioned. He decided to throw her an answer that might satisfy. "She goes by Miss Freddie with her students. That's all." He wasn't going to give Dianne more.

"Okay." She drew out her one-word response over several seconds.

"Look. I've got to go. We've got a burning house, a displaced couple, and a gang of troublemakers on the run. I'll check in later." He slammed down the phone, disgusted for giving the office manager something to romanticize about. The woman often tried to set him up with someone for a blind date. His wife had been perfect for him. He had family and a witness to protect. He stalked out of the barn and spotted Winifred, not Freddie, sitting between two medics. His steps faltered. Had she been hurt when they fled the house?

<p style="text-align:center">~~~~~</p>

Freddie watched Kent rush across the yard to where she sat in the back of the ambulance. Other than a few scrapes from her fall, she was unharmed. Heat rushed up her neck as Kent's gaze roamed over her bandaged elbows and knees. Maybe somewhere deep down, he still cared about her. Then again, maybe he only cared for the safety of his witness.

"I'll live. Now it's your turn for an examination of your head." She pointed to his bleeding forehead. Her half-smile suggested a double meaning about his hard head.

He touched the area with a finger and winced. "I'm fine."

Freddie raised an eyebrow. "Why don't we let these medics check it out anyway?"

She heard Kent mutter under his breath, but he sat still while the EMTs cleaned his head wound and sealed it with butterfly bandages. They also covered a few burns on his arms with a cooling gauze wrap and recommended he follow up with a doctor for a prescription cream or possible antibiotic. He nodded, but Freddie wondered if he would do anything about it until he finished his business with her.

Her mind wandered to her own business ventures as she walked over to lean on a fence near the barn. Teaching had been her life for close to two decades. She loved her students and the profession. Could she keep her position or would no one hire her once they discovered she was part of a federal case, which she could have prevented by making a smarter choice in the past? She hadn't been the best secretary, based on working for MAX Enterprises. Clerical skills no longer interested her as a career option.

That left her artistic endeavors. Very few people knew about her activities as Winnie Gee, author and illustrator of children's books. She might still be able to keep supplying picture books somewhat anonymously, but it was a supplemental income at best. Her thoughts roamed back to what she'd been working on when Amber and the federal agents arrived at her cottage. Had the criminals discovered her secret passion and ruined that income too? Would the current pursuit and eventual trials make it impossible to continue creating or meet her next deadline? There were so many unanswered questions. She closed her eyes and faced the morning sun, praying for peace to face an uncertain future.

"What's on your mind?" Kent's voice took her by surprise.

Freddie opened her eyes and placed a hand on her chest. She wasn't usually this jumpy, but she had an excuse after being on the run for what seemed like forever. Had it only been a couple of days?

"I was thinking about my future or lack thereof. Am I going to be able to go back to my magpies at school? Will I be in a safe house forever? Can I ever work with children again as a teacher or author and illustrator?" Freddie stopped her ranting when Kent got a strange look on his face. "What?"

"When we left your home, I asked you about Winnie Gee and you never answered me. Are you living another lie?" A frown marred his face.

She crossed her arms. "Plenty of authors and illustrators use pen names on their work. There's nothing illegal about that. I wanted my art students to respect me as their teacher and not as a well-known picture book creator. Besides, I didn't want Max to know about that part of my life. It was enough that he knew I was teaching."

Kent's eyes met hers. His frown softened into a winsome look, making her heartbeat pick up its pace. "So you really are Winnie Gee?"

"Yes, but I'd prefer you kept that fact to yourself since it may be my only career option in the future." She took a deep breath, praying he'd honor her request.

"On one condition. My grandkids love your work. I hope you will autograph their Winnie Gee books once this case is over."

His half smile lifted a burden from her shoulders. "I'd be glad to autograph everything they have as long as no one screams favoritism or conflict of interest against either of us."

"We won't speak of it until this case is over and we're free to visit as friends."

Freddie couldn't stop her lips from curling upwards. "I'd like for you all to come and visit me. I welcome friends to my house."

"I'd like to be your friend again." He moved closer, then hesitated before stepping away. He placed his hands on his hips. "Once this case has gone to trial, I think friendship will be a good place to start. For now, I'm going to see if our fellow captives, J.P. and Sarah Patterson, can provide any other information about the criminals."

Freddie relaxed against the fence post. He'd offered a chance for a new beginning, if they survived long enough for that to happen. Kent was smart to put the conditions on their relationship, but she couldn't stop hoping for that day to come sooner, rather than later. She'd missed Kent. He'd been her only romance.

Though he offered friendship, deep down she couldn't help but wonder about a renewal of the past. She thanked the Lord that he'd brought up their ham sandwich dates. If she hadn't been free to help untie Kent, it was obvious that the rough group of men wouldn't have come back to rescue them.

A low whimper sounded from the nearby barn. When she and Kent had walked across this field they'd heard a dog. She realized now that she'd not heard barking again. She followed the whining until she reached a closed stall. Peering over the half-door, she spotted a chubby basset hound with its head sticking out of a blanket bound with duct tape. The dog's mouth hung open and drool dribbled from its tongue. It looked half-asleep.

Freddie pulled the door open and knelt by the hound. It gave a half-hearted woof as she freed it from the blanket and tape. Once she'd released the dog, it staggered to the barn door and let loose with a tremendous howl. The poor beast would make a good character in a picture book, if it survived whatever was making it tipsy.

The dog wobbled toward Sarah Patterson, who rushed away from J.P. and Kent. Then she sat on the ground and hugged her pet. "Sweet Cakes, what have they done to you?"

Freddie described the condition she'd found the dog in and suggested a vet visit might be in order. One of the volunteer firemen, a family friend of the Pattersons, offered to take the dog in for a check-up so the couple could tend to the business of their destroyed home.

A few minutes later, a dark SUV rolled into the driveway. When two men stepped from the vehicle, Freddie watched Kent check their identification. He nodded and turned to wave her over.

Her heart sank as she headed toward the future. Would the next step in their journey take them down separate paths? That might be for the best, but it wasn't what she wanted.

Chapter Nine

Kent held the SUV's rear door open for Winifred. He needed to keep her legal name in his mind and not keep reverting to Freddie. Her eyes didn't meet his. He hated to admit that it felt like a relief. Their relationship would need to be business-related until the case against MAX Enterprises wrapped up.

He'd hoped for two vehicles, but the agents explained that only one car had been available. They'd travel to the safe house first. By mid-afternoon, other agents would join them and assume protection of the witness.

It would take about an hour to reach the isolated cabin, according to the agent climbing into the driver's seat. Once they'd hidden her away, Kent would be free to head into the local headquarters and make contact with his agents and possibly family on secure lines. Checking on his grandchildren's safety weighed heavily on his mind as he walked around the SUV and settled into the backseat next to his witness.

The agent standing outside the car scanned the area and then settled into the passenger seat. "The area looks secure. Let's take the rural roads, just in case."

"Enjoy the ride, folks. It looks like we're taking the scenic route, so it might take a little longer to get to our destination." The driver put the car in gear and introduced himself. "I'm Jared Sutter and this is my buddy, Paul Boling."

"Thanks for coming guys. As Agent Russell has probably informed you, I'm Winifred Grimsley, witness to a cybercrime." Her voice weakened by the time she'd finished talking. A yawn escaped. She was probably exhausted.

Kent fought the desire to join his yawn with hers. He watched as she closed her eyes and gnawed on her lips. He needed a distraction. "Did you bring the burner phone I asked for? I need a new weapon and badge too."

Paul reached into the console and pulled out a non-descript smart phone and a weapon in a shoulder holster. "Here you go. The phone's pretty basic but should provide good communication in an emergency. I'm sure you know the drill about not using any identifying information."

"Thanks." Kent leaned forward enough to put the weapon in place. He opened the phone and linked to an online free paper for a community near where his grandchildren lived. He scrolled to the classified notices and spotted a message reading, 'tell Poppy K we love him.' Good, that part of his family was safe for another day. His thoughts turned to their former foster child. The temptation was strong to contact Dianne and make sure she had followed up with protection duty, but the reminder about phone protocol held him in check. He trusted his office assistant to complete the assignment and didn't dare risk having someone tracking him as the user of the phone. He closed his eyes and allowed his exhaustion to lull him into a state of guarded rest.

<div align="center">~~~~~</div>

Kent's head swayed from side to side as his mind slowly returned to full awareness. Tall forests covered the terrain on either side of the road. Jared's driving had slowed to accommodate the curving pavement as it climbed higher up the side of a mountain. When they left the pavement and headed onto a gravel drive, Kent straightened and rolled his shoulders.

Winifred lifted her head from where she'd been slumped. "Are we there, yet?"

"Your home away from home is just ahead, Miss Grimsley," Paul announced. "However, we'll need to give the surroundings a routine check before we move you in."

She placed a hand on her middle. "I hope you are moving in some food. I'm starved."

"The place is usually well-stocked with canned goods, but we did grab a couple of fresh items. There's also some loose-fitting adjustable clothes and toiletries in one of our bags, courtesy of Agent Angela Carpenter."

"Tell Agent Carpenter that I'm grateful for thinking of those things." A brief smile crossed Winifred's face, sending a long-forgotten feeling of attraction across Kent's chest.

Looking away, he scanned the area as Jared pulled into the clearing, circled the yard, and pointed the SUV back down the driveway for a possible quick escape.

Paul turned to Kent. "Do you want to stay with the car or help secure the area?"

"I'll stay here with my witness." Kent stepped out of the car and stood at attention near the driver's door. Jared dropped the key fob into his hand and began walking the perimeter. Paul headed for the cabin, circled it, and then entered through the front door. Several moments later the men returned to the car and began removing bags from the trunk.

"We're all clear. Let's get this in and get some lunch going. Angela must have had you in mind. She insisted we take this cooler full of deli sandwiches when we left this morning."

Kent's stomach growled at the mention of food. "I wonder if there are any ham sandwiches."

Freddie's laughter entered his ears. It was a good thing she could look back on their morning adventure and not be screaming. The other agents looked puzzled until Kent explained the connection to their near catastrophe and how Winifred was free to make ham sandwiches and help save him from the ticking bomb.

After filling up on sandwiches, chips, and green grapes, Winifred headed to the shower with the bag of toiletries and fresh clothing, leaving the men free to talk business for a while.

"Once our replacement agents arrive to protect Ms. Grimsley, we can take you to the Roanoke headquarters so you can check on the progress of your team." Jared leaned back in an easy chair and propped his feet in the air.

"Our supervisor is requesting an additional agent to work with you while you're in our area." Paul walked to the cabin door and looked through a peephole in what looked like a wooden door. Kent had noticed a heavy metal clunk of reinforced material when he'd bumped into it while bringing in bags. The cabin was a fortress in disguise. Even the glass in the windows looked extra thick.

Thank the Lord, for providing a safe place for his witness. Now he could leave her in protection while he searched for Marcus, Alexander, and whoever else was part of the cybercriminal group that seemed to know how to follow Max's daughter, Amber, across country.

The sound of running water stopped and a few minutes later Winifred entered the room wearing sweatpants and a tee-shirt. Her hair was turbaned in a towel. She looked beautiful and refreshed. Kent swallowed as he squashed old feelings and yearned for new ones.

"I'm going to claim a bedroom and try to rest. It feels good to not smell like a fire anymore. You should get cleaned up while you have the chance." She wagged a finger toward Kent, making him feel like one of her students.

"You're right." He took off for the shower before he said anything personal out loud. By the time he finished cleaning up and switching to his own pair of sweats and shirt, the casual atmosphere in the main room of the cabin had changed.

Paul checked his watch and paced near the front window.

"What's wrong?" Kent watched the man's agitation grow.

"Since we took the scenic route and our replacements planned a quicker path, they should have arrived by now."

Jared frowned. "Maybe they got stuck in traffic. Someone will let us know if there's a problem."

"Aren't we supposed to be radio-silent out here?" Kent asked.

"That's the plan unless..."

Paul interrupted Jared's comment. "Quiet. I think I hear a vehicle."

~~~~~

Freddie's eyes popped open as a door slammed shut. The conversation outside her room included a female voice. She crawled out from under the warm blanket and shook her head, trying to wake from her short nap. Too bad this whole thing wasn't a nightmare. The dimly lit log-reinforced walls and rumble of voices from the other room confirmed the current reality.

She and Kent were on the run from cybercriminals who wanted them dead or alive. Make that, they wanted her dead or alive and were threatening Kent's family to find her. Guilt over the past made her teeth grind for a moment. She slipped sock-clad feet into her travel-worn shoes, took a deep breath, and walked toward the main room of the safe house.

As her door squeaked open, Kent stood and stepped forward. He took her elbow and led her into the space occupied by four agents. He waved toward the two new faces. "This is the witness, Miss Winifred Grimsley. She worked for MAX Enterprises many years ago when the company first strayed from running a clean business. Her testimony will be important after one of my agents collects a series of clues needed to solve this case."

The woman nodded. "It's nice to meet you, Miss Grimsley. I'm Angela Carpenter. My partner Evan Reach and I are from the Roanoke office here in Virginia. We'll be staying with you for the next few days." She lifted two stuffed backpacks. "I brought several more choices of clothing for both of you. The ones I sent this morning were what we had on hand."

"Thank you, Angela, for everything. I'll appreciate having some fresh changes of clothing. You and Evan may call me Freddie." Kent's grip on her arm tightened and then released as he stepped back, waving her toward a couch. Everyone found a seat. The warmth of Kent's body comforted Freddie on one side, while the petite Angela sat to her right.

Paul sat on the edge of a single chair facing the new agents. "What took you so long? We were beginning to think you ran into trouble since you're almost two hours later than we anticipated."

Evan leaned forward. "May we speak freely in front of Miss Grimsley?"

Kent nodded. "She knows as much as we do, if not more, about those who are after us."

Freddie sat up straighter. Kent's trust lifted her spirits. A trickle of relief flowed through her veins as she faced Evan.

"Actually, there was trouble. Someone started following us not long after we left headquarters. We tried to give them the slip. After several attempts, we went back to the office and left in a different vehicle. Two
~~~~~

other agents drove our original car on a decoy route. We took a circuitous course to get here so we wouldn't attract a tail." Evan's gaze shifted from Jared, to Paul, to Kent as he relayed more details about the treacherous journey on the gravel road that brought them to the safe house. "Paul and Jared may want to transport Agent Russell out, using that passage."

A sense of loss filtered into Freddie's heart. She knew Kent planned to leave her at the safe house. That was the best plan to facilitate her safety and his search for the two men threatening her. The departure would soon become reality. She sighed and forced acceptance into her mind. She'd faced disappointment more than once in her life.

"How soon will they need to leave?"

Kent's face sobered. "I'd like to go as soon as possible."

Jared looked toward a window. "The sun's almost down. We'd be safer waiting until morning in order to stay on twisty roads without guardrails."

Paul added, "Our headlights would light up the mountainside and might draw the enemy to the location of the safe house."

Angela laughed. "Besides, I promised this crew I'd fix my secret chili recipe before they left for town. We thought it might be for the mid-afternoon meal, but it looks like it will make a tasty supper instead."

Kent frowned. The other three men smiled.

Freddie stood and rubbed her hands together. "What can I do to help prepare the food?"

Angela joined her and looped their arms together. "How are you at grating cheese? The store was out of the shredded kind."

"I'm pretty good at shredding things." The men grew quiet. "I meant shredding cheese, guys. I never shredded any evidence. I just ran away."

Freddie thought she heard Kent murmur something under his breath about running from his shredded heart. He had that right. If only she'd made a different choice. Too many reminders of the past were going to make it easy to see him take his leave in the morning. Weren't they?

She plodded toward the kitchen. At least the men would be happy to bite into their shredded cheese and special recipe chili.

"What was that all about?" Angela opened a cooler and laid out fresh tomatoes, ground beef, a hunk of sharp cheddar cheese, a variety of fresh peppers, an onion, and several spice containers.

"What are you talking about?" Freddie hoped Angela hadn't heard what she thought was only in her imagination.

"Did you shred Agent Russell's heart?" Angela waved a knife in the air before spearing it into a tomato top.

"I guess I wasn't hearing things." Freddie wanted to squirm or go hide in her room.

"Nope. Spill the beans, Winifred. What did Kent Russell mean by his comment a few minutes ago?" Angela laughed as she lifted a can of black beans from a grocery bag.

"Well, I did break his heart, but I thought it was for his own good." Freddie paused and Angela circled a hand through the air indicating she should continue.

Freddie looked away before deciding to spill her guts. Angela seemed like a nice person. Hopefully the woman wouldn't hate her after hearing the whole story. "We were seriously dating. Unfortunately, around that time I discovered discrepancies at MAX Enterprises and confronted my boss. He said if I wanted to see my boyfriend live, I wouldn't report anything to the authorities. I like to think I saved Kent's life. I thought the only way to keep us both safe was to disappear, using a special buyout from Max Whitney. Kent calls it blackmail on my part. I just wanted us both out of danger." A slight headache started to hammer on Freddie's temples. "Now, we're still in danger despite all my big attempts to escape trouble."

Angela pulled a plastic cheese grater from her supply bag and held it out to Freddie. A slight smile crossed the agent's face. "Based on the few moments I've seen you two together, I think he still cares. I have a feeling you do too." She wiggled her eyebrows at Freddie. "Now why don't you give this grater a rinse and start shredding cheese instead of dripping tears into my recipe."

"I wasn't crying." Freddie might have given it a thought, but hadn't given in.

"No, but you will in a few minutes when I put you in charge of dicing the onion."

Chapter Ten

Freddie choked as she sat straight up in bed. She'd made a big mistake. A wind raged outside her window and inside her throat. She should have known better than to eat the fiery chili so late in the evening. Now her stomach was wreaking vengeance on her esophagus. She needed a quick remedy. Heading to the kitchen was her only choice, unless she wanted to end up retching the rest of the night. If she remembered correctly, Angela's provisions included several choices of soft drinks, including ginger ale. Freddie coughed violently. She rushed for the kitchen.

"Miss Grimsley, are you all right?" Lightning flashed as one of the male agents stood from his posted seat by a window.

Great. No private moments in federal protection.

"I just need something for heartburn. I think I saw some ginger ale." Rawness in her throat made her voice scratchy. She reached into Angela's cooler and grabbed the drink. A few sips of the bubbly soda and several raucous burps later, her throat began to clear.

"I've got some antacids in my bag. I always carry them for when Angela serves her chili. Would you like one?"

"Thanks, Evan. I'd really appreciate that, if you don't mind." She recognized the agent now that he stood under the bright light in the rustic kitchen.

"I'm happy to share. I'll be back in a second." Thunder boomed and the ground shook. Evan returned with a bottle of familiar pink pills. "That sounded close."

She shook a pill out of the bottle and chewed the chalky over-the-counter remedy. She'd still need to sit up for a while, but both the drink and the medication were helping.

Another long-lasting rumble split the air. Lights flickered. Darkness enveloped the cabin. A glow from Evan's phone filled the room with shadows.

"You might as well get back to bed and try to sleep if you can. I'll light a path for you."

"Thanks again." She followed as they wove their way through the building. After making it back to the edge of the bed, she watched Evan shut her door. A flash of lightning lit the room, immediately followed by another loud bang and a crash. Sleep wasn't going to happen anytime soon.

It didn't sound like anyone else had sleep on their minds. Several voices filtered through the wall, but she couldn't make out what the agents were discussing. She waited for a flash of lightning and then tip-toed to her door. It cracked open without a sound, enabling her to listen to their conversation.

"The weather maps have this storm dissipating around daybreak. We'll plan on leaving as soon as possible. Kent will go with us back to Roanoke. Evan and Angela will stay here with Miss Grimsley until we hear otherwise."

She pushed the door closed and returned to her bed. They were sticking with the plan. Stacking her pillows against the headboard, she leaned back in a half-sitting position. Praying for rest and safety brought some comfort as she finally dozed into a restless slumber.

~~~~~

Hours later, a ray of sun streaming through a gap in the curtain woke her. The slight scent of burning wood and frying bacon beckoned her to get out of bed and face the day, a day without Kent. The agents' plans to leave at dawn had come and gone. He hadn't even bothered to say goodbye. Freddie guessed that was payback for the time when she'd disappeared years ago. She pulled the curtains back, allowing light to fill the room. Grabbing the backpack of clothes provided by Angela, she headed to the bathroom to start her day.

Dressed in a fresh outfit, she followed her nose to the kitchen where Angela lifted a glass pan filled with bacon and scrambled eggs from the oven.

"Good morning, Miss Grimsley. I hope you like a hot breakfast. Hopefully it won't be too stiff from staying in the oven for a while. Would you like coffee, hot chocolate, or something else to drink?"

"Chocolate sounds delightful and you can call me Freddie." She closed her eyes and sighed.

"I can also put some bread in the toaster, Freddie." Angela lifted a bag of whole wheat slices.

"I didn't know toasters worked without electricity." Freddie's mind still felt hazy after the long night.

"The power's been on for several hours. We just needed to switch a breaker back on. How do you think the oven kept your food warm?" The agent poured hot water from a carafe into a cup and stirred in a chocolate mixture.

Freddie scrambled to make sense of her scattered thoughts. "I smelled burning wood when I woke up and assumed this doubled as a wood-burning stove. It looks kind of rustic." Freddie nibbled a piece of bacon and studied the kitchen in the morning sunlight. Even the refrigerator and
~~~~~

microwave doors had wooden panels covering them.

"Whoever designed this place wanted it to look that way, but it is fully electric. Maybe one of the guys started a fire in the fireplace last night while they were on duty and that made your nose work." Angela pulled the hot cocoa from the microwave and set it down with a flourish.

Freddie lifted a bite of eggs to her mouth. "Mmmm. These are not rubbery at all. Do I detect a little cheese in the mix?"

"Another secret recipe of mine, but don't tell Evan when he wakes up later. He hates cheese. I'm glad you're enjoying them though. What did you decide about the toast?"

"If you happen to have any honey, I'd love to have both." Freddie sipped some of her drink. The chocolate smell was strong, but she still thought the scent of burning wood filled the air. Maybe it was just the smell of singed bread coming from the toaster.

Freddie finished her meal and took her plate to the sink. The sound of a vehicle blowing its horn echoed across the mountainside. Angela drew her gun and rushed to peer through the front window curtains. Evan hopped from his room, pulling on his shoes. Freddie froze.

~~~~~

"Are you sure there's no other way out?" Kent held one hand over his free ear so he could hear above the noise of the tooting horn. They'd broken the request for cell phone silence when smoke and flames engulfed the only roads to and from the safe house. After calling into the Roanoke headquarters for a suggested next step, they'd left the encroaching forest fire and headed back to the cabin as fast as the twisting roads allowed. As they neared the building his phone rang with the latest information. "Okay, we'll do our best to make it there."

They skidded to a halt, jumped from the car, and ran for the door where Evan stood with his handgun at his side.

"What's going on? Are you trying to tell the world where we are?"

Kent held his phone in the air. "There's a forest fire blocking off any entrance or exit from our location. Your bosses at Roanoke suggested we hike to the top of the mountain. There's an area without trees where the forest service has room to land a helicopter. We need to get moving to keep above the fire. And hopefully keep ahead of the game in case any of our pursuers are listening to the rangers' chatter about rescuing us."

Evan stepped to the side and waved them in. "Did you hear, ladies?"

Angela pulled two backpacks from a closet and headed to the kitchen. "I'll get some water and snacks packed."

Freddie stepped from the bedroom holding a loosely filled bag. "I lightened the load in this pack. I have room for some supplies too."

"Good idea." Kent pulled extra clothes from his own pack and followed Freddie into the kitchen where they each added drinks and
~~~~~

snacks. He paused for a moment and faced Angela. "Have you or any of the agents hiked up this mountain before?"

"Both Evan and I have. It was part of our training to know this mountain well. We can direct you upwards, but it won't be an easy climb." She looked between Freddie and Kent, as if she was assessing their endurance.

Winifred lifted her chin. "I've done some weekend hikes around Lee County. I should be able to keep up with Kent."

Kent clamped his mouth shut. Living in the flatlands of Ohio hadn't prepared him for hustling up to the top of anything other than the stepper at his local gym. He hoped that was enough for him to keep up with the rest of the crew. He swung his loaded pack over his shoulder. "Let's move."

The other agents had rustled up enough walking sticks for each person and passed them out. Evan's pack had rope looped at the bottom and a couple of digging tools hanging from the side. Everyone fell in line. Evan and Angela led the way up the steep incline. Kent and Winifred followed. Paul and Jared took up the rear. Kent noted the two agents behind were scanning the surroundings. Good for them. He did his best to check things out, but concentrated more on not tripping over roots and forest debris littering their unmarked trail to higher ground.

Though there had been little rain from the late night storm, the dampened ground filled the air with a musty smell and made each step a potential slide backward. He'd already managed to embarrass himself with that move twice within the first fifteen minutes they'd been in the woods. Too bad the storm hadn't provided a deluge to keep the fire from spreading to the rapidly drying pine needles. The scent of the forest fire increased along with their measured breathing as they inched farther into the pine-filled woods.

An hour later, Angela called back to the others. "There's an outcropping of rocks just ahead. We'll take a break to grab some liquid."

Kent nodded, too out of breath to comment.

Winifred took hold of his arm. Her fingers tightened as she pulled him forward. He wanted to resist. Instead, he decided to enjoy the moment. Plodding along beside her felt right even when he tried to deny his interest in his former girlfriend.

"You can do this, Kent. It's only a few more steps." Her quiet words reached his ears. He picked up his pace, then felt a loss when she let go of his arm at their stop. "What a view."

He turned his gaze in the direction she faced. Clear skies above revealed an occasional cloud in a field of blue. Greens in various tints filled the mountainside below. Further down, pillars of smoke and flames billowed and belched as they encircled the bottom half of their vista. The fire was definitely moving their way. Kent pulled a bottle of water from his pack and guzzled it down. "We need to get moving again."

Evan nodded his agreement. "The next section's going to be a little tricky. There's a rock face between here and the top. We'll have to do some rock climbing. I'll go first and set an anchor to bring the rest of you up. If you're not agreeable to that, it will take the rest of the day to get above this area by walking the long way around." He paused and frowned. "I'm not sure we have that kind of time if the fire isn't controlled soon."

Kent slung his backpack over his shoulders. Energy flowed in his veins. He might not like hiking mountains, but he was great at climbing the rock wall in his gym back home. This time he was the one to grab Freddie's arm as they made their way toward the next step of their adventure. She trembled.

"Are you all right?" he asked.

"I am terrified of heights." Her voice shook more than her arm.

Chapter Eleven

Give her a class of sullen kids, or a stubborn administrator, or even a teacher in-service with a dry speaker any day, but climbing into the air without her feet on a solid slab of earth was another matter. Even glass elevators made her want to heave. Her thoughts wandered as they trekked closer to the looming wall of rock.

"I don't remember you being bothered by heights."

"I didn't have a problem with heights when we dated." She huffed.

"Do you want to talk about it?"

"No. Sure." She didn't really want to talk about it but knew doing so might give her something to do as they walked toward her fate. "My fear of heights started during my European travels and has grown over the years. I always wanted to climb the Eiffel Tower, so I visited it one day. I didn't anticipate the elevator cost and had only taken a small amount of money with me, due to the threat of pickpockets. Opting to climb the massive structure fit my limited budget better. Besides, I needed the exercise after sitting most of the previous day for a lecture at the Louvre."

Kent turned with a look of awe on his face. "You must have enjoyed seeing the art museum and the Eiffel all within the space of a few days."

Freddie looked down and focused on placing her feet on the upward trail. "I was excited about both places, but when I reached the tower's top, my legs wobbled like wet noodles from exhaustion. The view was amazing, but it sent more than an awestruck thrill through me. I gasped when looking down through glass panels as the world seemed to sway."

"You were probably tired from your climb." Kent's attempt at consolation didn't help.

"I thought so too. I lingered at the top and purchased a small seltzer drink to calm my stomach. Each step down grew scarier. A wind picked up. At one point a gust knocked me against the railing. I fell down and twisted my ankle. I limped down to the elevator at the next level and an attendant let me slip in for a ride down."

"I'd call that a blessing," Kent said.

"It might have been, but as I grasped a side rail my stomach squeezed. The glass windows of the elevator only reinforced my growing terror, even though the car traveled slowly. I tried closing my eyes, but it only made the sensation of falling worse. Somehow, I managed to keep from spewing all over the others until I left the elevator."

She widened her diaphragm and whooshed out a breath as her thoughts returned to the present. Warmth filled her as Kent wrapped his arm around her shoulders for a moment and then removed it after a slight squeeze. She felt the loss until he grasped her hand and led her up the trail.

"What other places did you go while you were in Paris?"

He was good at distracting her. She could deal with that. Her breathing returned to normal. "The art museums were amazing, especially the Louvre. The Mona Lisa was amazing. During one of my art history classes we had an amazing tour of Versailles. The wall-sized portraits were awe-inspiring. We also did plein-air painting when our class traveled to Chantilly."

"You painted with air?" He chuckled.

"No, we went outside and painted landscapes of the town and countryside near the Chantilly castle." She'd kept the painting from that day, now hanging in her cottage. Hopefully her home still existed. She blinked, missing the place that served as her hideaway for years.

Kent stopped walking. When Freddie looked toward the others, they were pulling water bottles from their packs and staring at the rock wall standing between them and the mountain top.

"When this is all over, maybe you can come back and do one of those air paintings." Kent gave her hand a squeeze before releasing it and grabbing his own drink.

"Maybe you can take a picture with your phone, and I'll safely make a painting inside my studio room if we survive." Freddie guzzled half a bottle and turned around to look where they'd come from. Flames covered the mountainside below. Overcoming her fear was the only option for survival.

Evan clanked a couple of spikes together. "Everyone needs to watch me as I climb. There should be natural places to stop or hold. If there aren't any, I'll hammer in one of these pitons. After I reach the top, I'll anchor a rope that you will use for your safety. That way if you lose a handhold, I'll be able to pull you the rest of the way."

Freddie wanted to look away, but she forced her eyes to follow Evan's every move. Her stomach churned when he paused to pound in a spike with his hammer. Moments later a loop of rope dropped over the side. Paul secured it around his chest and made a slow ascent. Angela scrambled up next like a professional climber. Two ropes tumbled downward.

Jared moved closer. "Miss Grimsley, you're up next. I'm coming right behind you. If you slip, I'll be right there to stop you from falling. I've had experience assisting new climbers."

"What about Kent, I mean Agent Russell? Shouldn't he go next?" She wanted to put off the inevitable as long as she could.

"No, we need an armed agent to come up last. Isn't that right, sir?" Jared faced Kent.

"Agreed. I'll see you at the top." Kent nodded as he looked into her eyes. "You've got this. Don't look down." He helped tie the rope and leaned close to her ear. "Let God give you strength."

Jared waved her ahead. They began their climb. Saying a prayer of her own, she stared at the wall and didn't look back, making the climb easier than she thought it might be. She could hear the large man's breath and feel it warm her pant leg as he puffed along behind her. The smell of moist soil filled her nose as her hands gripped the gritty textures of the cliff.

The hardest part was crawling over the wall's top. Her heart flipped as Angela dragged Freddie's upper body across the edge. Her legs flailed in empty air as she attempted a scream that refused to form. Her foot connected with something. Jared groaned as Angela pulled Freddie forward over the rough ground.

"You made it, friend. Now let's get you untied so we can send for your buddy down there." Angela loosened the rope and smiled.

Jared scrambled into view. A red mark on one cheek verified her foot's contact with his face. "Remind me not to get in range of your kicking feet."

"Sorry." Freddie sat up and scooted farther away from the precipice. She trembled in relief, not fear. *Thank You, Lord.*

Angela coiled one of the ropes while Jared hurled the second one over the cliff. The other men lined up, ready to haul Kent up the cliff. Jared held onto the rope and leaned forward.

"Are you ready down there?" Jared paused to listen. "Okay, keep the rope tight with a little give."

Freddie watched the men as she prayed for Kent's safety. A cry rang out. The men leaned back and braced their feet. Loose gravel slid under their feet as the rope pulled them toward the edge.

Freddie gasped. The anchor tree bent forward but stayed rooted in the soil. The rope tightened. The agents stopped sliding. She held her breath and begged God for Kent's life.

Jared moved onto his belly and peered over the edge. "How's it going down there?"

"I've been better, but I'm hanging in there, so to speak," Kent answered.

Jared inched closer to the edge. "See if you can swing toward the wall."

"I always wanted to fly." A tremor shook Kent's voice.

"Please, Lord, keep him safe." Freddie continued to pray as she watched the rope swing from side to side. Once it went slack, she released a big puff of air.

"I'm back in climbing mode. Thanks for the lift, guys." His voice echoed upwards.

Angela's hand squeezed Freddie's shoulder. "It looks like your prayers have been answered. Your hero is going to make it up the cliff. "

Freddie nodded but kept praying until Kent rolled over the edge to safety. The men exchanged high fives and pats on the back. Jared coiled the last rope while the others sipped water and shared stories about climbing other rock faces.

Her fear of heights finally kicked in. Delayed trembling shook Freddie's body. Her teeth chattered. She closed her eyes. At least she hadn't reacted while they were hauling her up. Warmth crossed her shoulders as Kent sat next to her and wrapped her in a sideways hug. She felt, rather than saw, Angela move away. The female agent probably thought there was something between the couple. There had been at one time for sure. There might be in the future, but who knew?

"Look at the sky. There are some nice clouds out there." His voice was reassuring.

She heaved a breath. Her shoulders shook less. "Thanks for the distraction."

"Glad to help. The mountaintop isn't much farther. Once we reach the summit, we'll helicopter out of here to a safe place."

"I'm not sure about riding in a helicopter." The idea actually frightened her, but she decided not to admit her fears. Their lives were more important.

"Close your eyes and pretend you're taking a plane to Europe." Did his voice hold regret about not being there for her during that time?

She swallowed the discomfort inching up her throat. "Planes are enclosed a little better than a helicopter. Besides, I was younger and braver when I went overseas." She let out a nervous chuckle.

"I think you've been pretty brave during this whole escape. I can tell from your voice that you're calm enough to move now." He reached into his backpack and held out a drink.

She took the bottle of water he offered. Moving on sounded like a great idea. Smoke still scented the air, and she longed for a safe place. After a few sips, she stood and faced away from the cliff. "I'm ready to hike the rest of this mountain."

"Great." He reached for her hand and pulled himself up with minimal reliance from her grip.

She turned to look directly at him for the first time since his rescue. The re-opened gash on the side of his head dripped blood. "Your wound needs to be re-cleaned and bandaged." She looked at the other agents. "Did anyone bring a first aid kit?"

Paul pulled one from a back pocket of his pack and handed it to Angela. Something uncomfortable crossed Freddie's mind as she watched the female agent attend to Kent's needs. The woman demonstrated skills beyond Freddie's limited experience. At work, school nurses usually took care of anything other than passing out bandages.

Watching Angela's capable fingers applying antibiotic cream and butterfly bandages made a sliver of jealousy filter into Freddie's thoughts. She turned and looked away. Kent had indicated a possible future, but a guarantee might not occur based on all that had happened in the last few days. Getting to the top of the mountain should be her priority at the moment, and not some imagined future. She shouldered her backpack and walked to where the male agents conferred.

"I just tried to make contact, but either this satellite phone is malfunctioning or something is interfering with the signal." Evan clipped the heavy device to his belt. "No worries. I know the way to our rendezvous point. We need to move out. The rescue team will arrive before we do if we don't hurry."

"Then let's go." Kent joined the group while Angela repacked the medical kit. They all fell in line in the same order as before, with the exception of Paul moving to the rear.

Freddie fought to keep her balance as the trail grew more rugged. Roots, vines, and animal waste littered the path. Foraging above the tree line would not provide much food for whatever creature had blazed the trail. Distant whirring split the silence as they neared the mountaintop. Those at the front of the line crested the ridge and moved out of sight. Relief was within reach. She increased her pace to keep up with those ahead of her. Her foot snagged on a root. She fell forward. Sticky brown scat covered her hand. A musty stink made its way to her nose and she fought a gag reflex as she swiped at the ground in an effort to clean her fingers.

"Are you all right?" Kent bent down next to her.

"I have a fistful of nastiness to deal with." She held out her hand, and then looked away.

Paul joined them. "Hold on a second and I'll get some wipes from the first-aid kit. We'll get you clean."

Paul offered her the antibacterial cloths. After using several, she felt better. When she looked at the men, their faces reflected worry. "Is something wrong?"

"It's too quiet. We should still be hearing the helicopter." Kent turned his head to one side as if listening.

Paul nodded. "I don't see the rest of our agents either. This doesn't feel right."

Chapter Twelve

Kent looked for a place to secure Freddie until he and Paul could figure out what was going on. The whirring of helicopter blades had vanished. Their team should be talking. Instead, silence reigned. He spotted a boulder surrounded by scrub bushes. It would have to do since they were above the tree line. He nodded to Paul. His fellow agent crouched low and approached the crest of the mountain.

Grabbing Freddie's hand, he fled with her toward the huge stone. Once they reached the protective cover, Kent motioned her down. She didn't argue, taking a squatting position instead of sitting. Winifred was a savvier woman than she'd been in the past. He brushed off his returning attraction and peered around the side of their limited fortress.

Paul neared the top. As his head cleared the summit another man sprang into view. A struggle ensued. Then a second man appeared and kicked Paul's feet out from underneath him and fired a taser. The agent squirmed on the ground as they wrapped rope around his body. It looked like the rope from their earlier climb. The criminals must have taken it from Evan's pack.

A voice echoed across the barren landscape. "You might as well give up, Winifred. We've captured all the feds, except for your old boyfriend. I don't think you can escape."

Kent barely heard Winifred whisper, "It's Marcus," as she touched his hand.

"I only see one place you could be hiding down there, and I've got my men circling around behind you. If you make a run for it, they'd be happy to end this here and now. But we recently figured out there's one more secret you need to share before we tie this up for good. You're going to help us buy our ticket out of this mess."

Kent looked at Winifred. She shook her head and looked confused. Obviously, they thought she knew something they didn't. That information, or lack thereof, might keep them alive for a while. Crunching footsteps approached from three sides. He and Freddie stood with raised hands. Rough men patted them down and removed his weapon. The criminals held guns to their backs and prodded them forward as they hiked up the slope.

When they passed the top, Kent took in the devastation. The team of agents lay on the ground, some in worse shape than others. In addition, two men in flight suits sat tied to the landing gear of the helicopter. Their faces were battered. Blood dripped from one of the airmen's lips. The man lifted his chin in defiance at the criminal standing over him.

"Tie the agent up with the others. Put Winifred over there alone. We'll want to move out of here once we find the key to this helicopter." Marcus glared at the pilots.

Kent glanced at the pilots. Helicopters didn't usually have keys. One of the battered men looked Kent in the eye and gave a tiny shake of his head before returning Marcus' glare.

"After you forced your way on and commandeered our ride, we had to take any measure we could to stop you. Throwing the key out right before we landed was one way to ensure you wouldn't get away with whatever crime you committed. Watching the key drop down that cliff made it hard to find." He laughed. "It won't be long before our superiors realize we haven't returned with the agents and their witness."

A slap knocked the pilot's head to the side. Kent bit back a retort, figuring it would only make things worse. At least the airman had given them time to work on a strategy. The rope coiled around Paul's body gave him an idea. "Evan is an excellent climber, maybe you should send him down the cliff to look for the key."

Marcus laughed. "I'm no dummy. You want your man to escape and bring in reinforcements."

Kent had hoped for that very thing. "Then, I guess we wait for those reinforcements to show up when the helicopter doesn't return on time."

"I'm sure the forestry men are too busy fighting the fire to notice one missing helicopter." A smirk crossed his face. "Nature and a little aid from some of my hired help will keep that blaze going for a while."

"And block any chance of escaping from this mountaintop." Kent stared at the evil man who seemed to be thinking.

"I'll find a way or maybe the forest rangers will douse the flames by the time we get off this mountain. In the meantime, I intend to discover what your old girlfriend knows about a certain pass code. Max set it up before his untimely death. If I get out of here alive, it may be the means to letting our departed boss take all the heat and keeping the rest of us safe from the long arm of the law." Marcus glared at Kent

"I'm afraid we've already got agents tracking down that information. Soon, we'll have everything we need to take your whole team of cybercriminals down." Kent didn't share that Marcus was already part of the investigation due to what Winifred shared.

"I heard his daughter Amber was helping the feds. It won't be long before we put an end to her little quest too." Marcus stomped across the rough terrain and leaned over Kent.

Kent jutted out his chin. "We know all about Martin being the mole you planted. He won't give us any more trouble." At least that was what he hoped. Though they'd figured out who the culprit was, the agency hadn't actually apprehended him. They hadn't located Martin's kidnap victim either.

Marcus smirked. "I think I know more than you on that account. Max's younger daughter, Jade, is easier to persuade. She's been very helpful to our cause."

Kent's fists tightened behind his back. If his bindings fell off, he'd welcome the challenge of subduing the maniac striding toward Freddie.

Marcus called over his shoulder. "Maybe Winifred Grimsley will be easily persuaded to share her secrets like Amber's little sister did."

~~~~~

Freddie watched as Marcus approached. His gaze bored into her. She forced her face into a mask, hoping it didn't show fear. The man had intimidated her in the past. That was before years of teaching and dealing with plenty of student attitude. Plus, she had no idea what he might be looking for.

The only contact with Max she'd had in the last few years was through the jewelry now in the possession of Amber and the federal agents who traveled with her. She blocked out Marcus' glare by closing her eyes and sending a plea to God. *Help me know what to say to this evil man. Help me answer in a way that will show You in my life. Protect those around me with Your caring hand.*

A grip on her chin broke her concentration, but not her connection to the Giver of Life. She looked at the eyes of her tormentor. "Have you ever thought of asking for forgiveness and changing your ways?"

Marcus stepped back like he'd been stung. His mouth dropped open for a second and then transformed into a sneer. "So you got religion since the last time we met. I don't need you preaching at me. I need answers. Do you have the code that Max gave you?"

"I have no idea what you are talking about other than a gift he sent me that is now in federal hands."

"Which federal hands? Did you give it to one of these agents or is it with Amber?"

"No one here has the gift." Freddie clamped her mouth shut. She'd practically told Marcus that Amber had the information.

She squeezed her eyes closed and tried to picture the box the jewelry came in. A sudden idea struck. Maybe it would distract the man without her having to lie. "I did keep the box it came in. There was wadded up paper in it. I didn't check to see if there was a code on the paper, but I guess it is possible."

Marcus nodded. "Did you keep the papers?"

Good, it looked like he might be taking her bait.
~~~~~

"I keep all my papers. They recycle into a pulp that I use for..." She clamped her mouth shut again. Marcus didn't need to know about her life as an author and illustrator who sometimes created her own handmade pages.

"Has it been recycled?" His voice held anger.

"No. It has been several months since I made pulp. I'm sure I could locate the papers if I looked. It might be hard to find since your partner Alexander blew up my front door." She plastered as much innocence as she could into her words and facial expression. "He obviously didn't find any clues about a hidden code. You're going to need me to find where I stashed those papers."

"But I won't need any of these agents." Marcus kicked Evan's side and the man groaned.

Freddie frowned. "If you harm them, the deal is off. Besides, you'd be in big trouble for shooting federal agents."

"Who said anything about shooting anyone? I'm going to leave them here to rot. If they happen to get help, then that is up to the fates or any wild animals looking for a meal."

"Then I'm not going." She pulled her lips into a pout.

Marcus nodded to two of his henchmen, who each grabbed one of her arms and lifted her to a standing position. "You don't have any choice."

"And how are you going to get us off this mountain without a helicopter?" Freddie shot a glare at Marcus.

"I'll take my chances with the fire." His voice didn't sound convincing.

"Two of these agents know the area. They might be of help. I'll also cooperate better if you bring Kent."

"Well, aren't we being helpful?" Sarcasm rolled from Marcus' voice. "If you get out of line, I can always threaten Kent in order to get your cooperation. I'll take that into consideration. Now tell me about these agents who know the area."

"Evan and Angela have hiked this mountain before. Evan is a skilled rock climber." She'd prefer that they take everyone, but would be happy to have any of the agents along.

"We'll take the woman agent. She won't be as big a threat as the man." His condescending look told Freddie that Marcus had definitely underestimated her new friend. She hoped Angela made him regret his comment sooner, rather than later.

Kent and Angela, each manhandled by a henchman, led the group toward the opposite side of the mountain from where they'd climbed earlier. Marcus grabbed Freddie's arm and followed them. The last two criminals brought up the rear. Both agents and Freddie still had bound hands, making them take slow careful steps. She had no desire to take another tumble into the gifts left behind by animals.

Remorse filled her about leaving the others behind, but she'd noticed Paul wink at her and then return to what looked like a tired slumber after his fight with the taser. It might have been her imagination, but it looked like the ropes around his body seemed looser than the ties binding the other men. When she'd first seen him, his shoulders had been wide to his side. In his fake slumber they now hunched inward toward his chest.

She didn't look back. No one needed to know what she'd seen, but hope filled her with courage to trudge ahead. Paul would wiggle out of his bindings soon enough. It wasn't by accident that she occasionally stomped her foot down, leaving a clear footprint in a patch of animal scat for anyone who might need to track their progress.

Chapter Thirteen

Kent looked to his side. Angela moved her hands closer together and then widened them. The plastic tie binding her hands together stretched slightly. Good. He'd been doing the same thing as discreetly as possible. The man beside him stumbled on the rough terrain and nearly fell, preventing the fall with one of the walking sticks they'd commandeered. The stick would make a good weapon once their hands were free.

"Better be careful, man. You'll end up rolling down the mountain if you keep stumbling like that."

The fellow glared at Kent. "I'm not worried about me. I figure the boss-man is going to send you flying as soon as he makes your woman talk." He poked at the ground in front of Kent, who stopped in his tracks.

"I've seen Marcus and Alexander betray some of their hired crew. It wasn't pretty. I wouldn't be surprised to see a repeat performance with you and your buddies. You guys got names?" Kent figured he'd gather intel in hopes of surviving.

"I'm not sharing with a Fed. I'm no dummy." The man resumed their trek forward.

Kent turned back toward Winifred and Marcus for a split second. "Then I'd keep your eyes open and not get outsmarted or burned. He did some burning with the last crew that tried to take us in."

His man ground out a curse under his breath. "Whatever. You need to close your mouth and keep walking."

Kent faced forward and concentrated on slowly stretching his ties. Sweat trickled from his brow and into his eyes. He lifted both hands to brush away as much moisture as he could. A hawk squawked, flying overhead toward the tree line. It wouldn't be long before they reached the shade. A light breeze rustled the trees. Then the wind-blown sound grew louder, much louder when the sound of rotors filled the air. He'd been right about helicopters not needing a key, other than for the door. Kent laughed.

"It looks like they didn't need a key after all."

The man holding his elbow dragged him into the trees. His companion did the same with Angela. Marcus and Winifred tumbled in behind them with the others. The helicopter hovered over the trees. It circled several times, as if searching for them. Then it turned and headed away.

"They may have fooled us, but it looks like we've turned the tables on them. Your hope of rescue is gone." Marcus yanked Winifred back to her feet.

"I'm sure they'll be back." Confidence filled Kent's voice. His captor pulled him forward into the forest. The roots became thicker and his companion tripped again.

Marcus jerked Winifred close. She cried out in pain."Your friends are leaving you behind for now. I'll still find a way to get that code before we see them again."

Kent wanted to deck the man. Instead, words spewed out of his mouth. "It won't do you much good. You've got a whole crew in that helicopter that can now attest to your involvement in kidnapping federal agents and our witness."

Marcus laughed. "I'll figure a way out of this. I've done it before. Now get moving."

"Ready when you are." Kent glared at Marcus and then glanced at Angela, who briefly shook her head. It wasn't time to act. His fellow agent would let him know when she was ready.

Angela groaned louder than necessary as her captor yanked her onto her feet. She spoke her next words in a whine. "Give me a while to get my bearings. There's rough terrain ahead. Someone might fall if we don't approach from the right angle."

Marcus frowned. "Quit trying to delay. Move out." He pushed Freddie forward.

After their travels resumed, Kent looked over his shoulder. "How are you doing back there, Miss Grimsley?"

"I'm making do. Do you think we'll see any bears today? That one I thought we saw the other day sounded ferocious." She rolled her eyes and moaned.

"Yeah, he was. He might be tracking us as we speak." The man beside Kent flinched. Winifred had found a crack in his armor. Kent found his own armor cracking wide-open. Freddie was an amazing woman. He'd missed her personality.

"If we step in the animal scat do you think the bear would lose our scent?" Desperation filled her words. Her drama skills were in top shape.

Kent held back a smirk. She'd gone from being totally repelled by the droppings, to using them to leave a trail of footprints. "That might work, but you're going to get awful smelly." He glanced over his shoulder again.

Marcus jerked Freddie closer. "This whole conversation stinks. Maybe I should leave Kent behind to satisfy the bear. Unless you're ready to share Max's code for his private documents, we need to keep moving."

"I don't think I'd share the code if I knew what it was. I really have no idea what you're talking about."

Good for her. Kent purposely stomped on a pile of rabbit pellets. His attendant didn't complain. They'd managed to plant an element of fear in at least one man's mind. Nature sounds abounded. Birds chirped. Breezes stirred the tree leaves. He noticed the man jump when they heard crunching nearby. Two deer darted away. The man's shoulders relaxed.

Seconds later, another cracking sound reached their ears. Kent laughed. "Those deer sure are noisy today." He heaved a big sigh, covering other sounds coming from his right side. He suspected that at least some of the agents had followed on foot.

Angela looked his way and nodded. She grumbled in a loud voice, "I need a break."

It was time.

Kent twisted away from his captor and brought his wrists down on one of his knees. The ties broke apart. He turned back to the man with his elbow flying. The man doubled over, rolled to the ground and kicked out at Kent's legs. They exchanged several punches and kicks before he knocked the fellow out cold.

Nearby, Angela's feet and arms flew as she attacked the man who had restrained her. Seconds later the guy held up his arms, surrendering to the highly trained agent. Jared had stepped from the woods and now hovered over Winifred, relieving her of the bindings holding her hands together.

"Where's Marcus?" Kent asked.

"Paul is in pursuit. At first we thought he was taking Freddie hostage, but he stepped behind a tree and pushed her aside. Paul and Marcus both took off running." As Jared pointed deeper into the trees, a shot rang out.

~~~~~

Freddie watched Kent hold up a hand for silence. The group complied, including the captives. Two more shots rang out, followed by rustling undergrowth. Someone ran, putting distance between them.

Paul's shout echoed back to them. "He winged me. I'm okay, but he's still out there with two of his henchmen."

Guilt threatened to overwhelm Freddie. "Now we have hidden enemies who will kill all of you until Marcus gets some code from me."

Jared pulled a device from his belt. "No worries. The helicopter is waiting for my satellite call. They'll be back in minutes to pick us up."

Freddie listened as he radioed the pilots and gave them the coordinates for picking up their group. She tensed when she heard someone or something moving in their direction. When Paul stepped from the woods with one hand raised, her shoulders relaxed.

"It's me, Paul. He got me. I might have given him a wound, but I couldn't tell."

Concern replaced fear as Freddie noticed blood trickling down his
~~~~~

other arm. Angela pulled the medical kit from Paul's backpack. Freddie assisted by handing cleaning wipes and bandages to the female agent. Moments later, they had his minor wound covered with a bandage. Paul applied pressure to the injured area while Angela packed up their gear.

"Thanks, ladies. If I ever need a doctor, I know who to call." Confidence returned to his voice as he stood and shook woodsy debris from his clothing.

"Speaking of needing a doctor, what happened to your other agent?" Kent asked.

"Evan really was injured during their takedown. He's in the copter." Jared searched the sky.

A whirring sound alerted Freddie to the incoming helicopter. "I think the cavalry has arrived." She stepped toward the open area.

Kent stopped her by wrapping an arm around her shoulders. "Wait until they land. We don't know if Marcus has his eyes on us. When the helicopter is settled, we'll make a dash together, with you in the center of our group."

Warmth rushed over Freddie as Kent tugged her closer. She enjoyed the protected feelings coursing through her, bringing back memories of their long-ago relationship. Max's mistakes in the past had pulled them apart. Could there be any hope for the future? In her dreams, possibilities danced. In reality, they would need to survive the dangers that Marcus and Alexander undoubtedly had planned before there would be time for a relationship.

The helicopter drew closer. Leaves, dirt, and twigs flew through the air and pelted them. Freddie turned away to protect her face from the stinging pieces. She nestled into Kent's chest. Both of his arms held her tight as his head bent down over hers. Warm breath whispered over her ears.

"I've got you, Freddie."

Did he really say that, or was her imagination playing tricks? If her ears weren't playing tricks, it sounded like Kent had called her Freddie. He stepped away, leaving her cold.

"Now's the time to run for the helicopter." He grabbed her hand. The others loosely surrounded them as everyone zigzagged from the cover of the trees toward their transportation. Freddie scrambled in first and headed for a back seat. The smell of metal, electronics, and oil brought back memories of some of the old radio parts Max had kept on display in his office. Before the man became a cybercriminal, he often reminded Freddie that Bell Lab's 1947 transistor opened doors to today's technology.

After Alexander, Marcus, and Victoria were hired, he rarely spoke of that interesting fact. Freddie had sometimes mentioned it to his young daughter Amber, when they played with the jars of transistors or glued them into artistic creations. She hadn't thought about the tidbit of information for years. Could the idea of opening doors with a Bell Lab 1947 transistor be the clue Marcus and Alexander were looking for?

Kent sat in the seat next to her, crowded in by the others since the helicopter carried more people than seats. She wondered if the cramped space affected his claustrophobia. He seemed tense. The grim look on his face was hard to read. He passed her a set of earplugs and donned a pair of headphones to cover the tremendous noise created as they lifted into the air and headed away from the mountain peak.

Her own phobia about heights kicked in for a moment, but she managed to force her thoughts to the magnificent scenery below and the handsome man leaning into her side. A slight curl in his short hair spiked around his headphone band. She took a moment to admire his face before focusing on the blues and greens covering the mountains. Sun-drenched patterns shifted colors across the sides of mountains and hills. Clouds drifted across the azure sky. Freddie memorized what she viewed as her thoughts turned to one day re-creating the scene on an artist's canvas, marred only by the fire and a circling plane spewing red fire-retardant chemicals. She wanted to share her inspiration, but speaking with the others would be impossible above the whirring rotors.

Gradually the mountains gave way to valleys and the helicopter prepared to land at a forestry service facility. Two men wearing neon vests waved orange batons as they guided the copter toward a landing spot. Freddie watched with interest as the craft slowly lowered and then bumped one last time onto solid ground. The rotors slowed. When Kent reached for her hand, her heart sped up. He didn't release his connection until they got the all-clear to disembark. She followed the others' examples and backed her way out of the flying machine. Putting feet back on solid ground felt great, though her legs wobbled beneath her. She could blame that on the flight or stress from the last few days. Either way, she was grateful when Kent offered her an arm as they followed the other agents toward a dark van with tinted windows.

Paul lifted his good arm and waved. "Hey, Smitty. I see they sent the limousine to pick us up."

"Ha ha. She's quite the vehicle, but I didn't think you deserved the real thing after running around in the woods all day." A middle-aged man, with gray streaks adorning his temples, held open the door and tipped his hat to the agents and Freddie. "Although, the limousine might be more appropriate for escorting a lovely lady." He smiled at Freddie as he lowered his hat to his chest and bowed. He held out a hand to assist her into the van.

She felt Kent stiffen at her side.

Chapter Fourteen

Kent pulled Freddie closer. "She's in my custody. I'll help her into the van." He may have lost her long ago, but he'd keep her close for now.

Smitty grinned and lifted his hands in the air. "Ah, I see how it is. You'll be happy to know I was just being courteous. I have a wonderful wife at home." The man had the nerve to chuckle as he offered his hand to Angela who was next in line. "How are you this fine day, Miss Angela?"

"I'm surviving. Thank you, Smitty. Did you have a good vacation last week?"

"The missus and I loved our trip to Alaska. The mountains and glaciers were amazing. We might go back on our next big anniversary."

Kent left the van seats behind the driver for the injured agents, Paul and Evan. He escorted Freddie to the middle and took the seat next to hers. He searched for a seatbelt with his head down. He'd stuck his foot in his mouth with regards to the driver. Maybe there was a chance she'd missed his comment.

Freddie snickered. "I look forward to this whole thing being over so we can see how things really are."

He smiled and leaned closer. "Me too. I'm glad you are safe. For now, we've got a long road ahead with two known criminals tracking us while their partner in crime, Victoria, is going after Max's daughter, Amber. The woman is probably behind the so-called kidnapping since she's the mother of Max's other child." He leaned away. "Hey, Smitty, do you have a secure phone I can use? I don't have confidence in the security of the one I've been using and I need to check in with my team."

"Sure thing, Agent Russell. Headquarters knew you'd want a fresh device." Smitty handed a phone back to the injured agents sitting in front of them. Evan groaned as he continued passing the cell on.

"I meant to get the device to you earlier, but you had other things on your mind." The man had the audacity to chuckle and wink as his grin beamed from the rearview mirror.

Several passengers coughed or cleared their throats. Angela giggled.

Kent shook his head and reached for the phone.

Dianne answered on the third ring. "Northwest Ohio Division, how may I help you?"

"Hey, Dianne, it's Kent checking in with yet another phone. I need an update on Graham's team."

"They've made it to Alabama and had a run-in with Victoria, Max's second wife. The woman is in custody. She insists she's not alone in this crime, but you've obviously met up with some of her cohorts."

"Yes, Alexander Johnson and Marcus Stanley are still on the run and threatening Winifred Grimsley. They've changed their focus from trying to kill her to seeing if she has some code to get them into Max's files. Was anyone else taken in with Victoria?"

"They arrested two other henchmen, including her son from another marriage. The team recovered Max and Victoria's kidnapped daughter, Jade. It turns out she was in Victoria's hands. While under duress, they forced Jade to give some hints about where our team planned to head next. The girl is excited to go home to Max's widow, who has legal custody. She also feels bad about telling about Amber's whereabouts, but Victoria threatened to harm a former nanny."

Kent's shoulders relaxed. "At least the information was coming from the child and not another mole."

"They haven't located our known mole, Martin, yet. Graham's team is looking for more of Max's clues on an Alabama mountain today. That's all I've got for now, Boss." Dianne's sigh resounded through the phone.

"Is anyone on duty to watch my foster grandchild, Melissa, in Forest Glen?"

"We're a little stretched for now, but the adoptive parents are aware of the situation. Ginny works part-time in the same elementary school where Melissa attends. She's spending her off hours volunteering in the girl's classroom. The father, Scott Hallmark, has a flexible schedule at the college and is doing his part to keep watch over Melissa and their other children. So far nothing is out of the ordinary. Are your grandchildren staying safe?"

"I'm going to contact them after I speak with the Roanoke office. For now, they are in hiding following a plan we laid out in case of an event like this. Thanks for the update." Kent disconnected the phone and watched the passing scenery. Rolling hills of pastureland mixed with plots of pine swept past his vision. Mountain peaks loomed in the distance. Freddie's shoulder slumped against his as her eyes closed and her breathing deepened. His breathing soon matched hers as he closed his eyes and prayed, thanking God for their safety thus far and asking for His guidance in any future he might have with Freddie.

Prayers for his grandchildren's safety reminded him to open the phone again and check the want ads in the agreed upon newspaper. A new message was there. The coded words indicated all was well, but the supplied food wasn't very popular. His grandchildren were older than the last time they'd gone to the cabin for a trip. Their eating habits had grown along with their bodies. They were probably yearning for a pizza or hamburgers instead of the rations of canned meat and vegetables stashed at the place. It was tempting to buy a pizza or taco kit and smuggle it in for them. They loved take-out food. He knew better, though. It wasn't worth risking their lives. He hoped they'd forgive him. Maybe meeting their favorite author, Winnie Gee, would someday make up for their lack of fast food. He closed his eyes and daydreamed of eating out with his grandsons.

The ringing of his phone interrupted his growling stomach.

"Hello?"

"This is Dianne. I just got a call from your son. He said one of the boys called and ordered pizza. He's afraid their hideout is no longer safe. Please call him right away."

~~~~~

Freddie couldn't help but hear snatches of the conversation between Kent and his son. Words like "alternate plan" and "meeting place" found their way to her ears as Kent physically turned away from her. After disconnecting the call, the gap between them widened as he slumped forward, his shirt tight against taut muscles, his elbows touching his knees. An aura of doom surrounded them.

The thought of reaching out and rubbing away his tension tempted Freddie. Knowing her actions had brought his family danger held her in place. She'd run away from him before and survived in hiding. Kent had a happy life without her complications. He'd have that once again. Stepping away was the right thing to do. Separation was already the plan. She should be glad to go their different ways and send him home to his grandsons.

Praying for strength, she opened her mouth and released her thoughts. "I'm sorry, Kent. After you hand me off to other agents to watch over me, I pray you and your family will no longer be in danger."

At first, he didn't reply. Then his head moved from side to side as he pushed back into a seated position. "You've been nothing but trouble for me from day one, Miss Winifred Freddie Grimsley. Your disruption in my life isn't going to stop whether we are together or on opposite sides of the universe. We may be distanced for a while, but don't count on the gap being permanent. With God's help, I plan to get you safely away from this situation, solve this case, and keep my family safe. Someday my grandsons are going to meet their favorite author and illustrator."

Freddie opened her mouth to argue, then clamped it shut. Warmth enveloped her as Kent closed the distance and leaned against her shoulder. She spoke no other words aloud. Instead, she closed her eyes and lifted prayers for God to cover them all with His hand.

A boom sounded at the same time Smitty yelled "gun." The van swerved from side to side. A screech blasted from Freddie's lips. How
~~~~~

could something else go wrong? Hadn't they been through enough? Smitty steered the slowing vehicle to the side of the road where it came to a bumpy stop, not far from an exit ramp.

Kent laid a hand on her arm. "Get down. This is too much of a coincidence. Did anyone see a reason for the tire to explode?"

"A car passed us right when the tire blew. I saw them point a weapon through their window." Smitty's angry voice grated in her ears as she slid from her seat. The other agents pulled their weapons and knelt on the floorboards.

"How did they find us?" Her voice shook. Grit covered her palms from the dirty floor covering.

"Your former employers are masters of the cyberworld. I'm sure they used technology." Kent faced the window with his weapon in hand.

Smitty snorted. "Or figured we'd be using this exit on our way to headquarters." He tapped a button on the steering wheel, starting a phone connection. One ring later someone answered. He didn't give them time to continue speaking. "Hey, it's Smitty. I'm south of the exit ramp near headquarters with the witness and four agents, tire's been shot out, and we're expecting trouble."

"I'll send the local police and some agents your way," a female voice replied.

The call ended. The back window shattered. Freddie lifted her head in time to see Angela level her gun on the top of the rear seat. She returned fire, then ducked below the sight line. Sirens sounded. Tires squealed. A vehicle sped away.

Freddie's legs started to cramp. She moved to climb back onto the seat. Kent waved her back down.

"Stay low until we give you the all-clear. Let the officials check outside before you put your head where anyone can see."

Crouching down wasn't as easy as it once was. She wanted to rear up like a horse and gallop away from this whole thing. Or trot. She still walked daily. Running had gone out of favor several years ago. Maybe she should jog her mind some more about what the code could be that Alex and Marcus thought she knew. She closed her eyes and let creativity flow. The one idea that came to mind earlier about the 1947 transistor could be a possibility. Maybe Max used his daughters' names or a favorite rock since he'd name the girls Amber and Jade. He'd bragged about how quartz had transformed electronics. His brass name plate had sat on the executive desk attached to a chunk of red granite. There were so many possibilities.

She crawled to the aisle near the van's sliding door and stretched out her legs. Tingling from blood flowing back into her legs drew her thoughts away from code words and back to Kent's nearness. His presence sent a different kind of feeling straight to her heart, one he'd hinted about exploring. Would they really be able to find a future? What would that mean to her teaching career? Sadness washed over her. She already missed her students. Her little magpies at school had become her family and children. Kent had his own family.

A rap on the door and a voice from outside indicated they were able to move from the van. Smitty's door squeaked open. Freddie scooted toward the side door as it slid away. Smitty stood waiting to assist her and the others to an older van waiting near the rear of their current ride. The shattered glass from the attack made Freddie shudder. Kent faced death every day. Could she live with that kind of worry on her mind?

She grabbed Angela's arm. "Sit with me for the next part of the ride."

Chapter Fifteen

Kent claimed the front seat of the van next to Smitty. Frustration whirled through his mind like a tornado as he clicked his seatbelt in place. Having the criminals chasing them didn't sit well with the way he wanted this case to play out. It was time to plan a new offense. Setting a trap had worked on Alexander a few days ago. It should work again with Marcus, based on the cocky man's attitude, but there were too many loose ends. Marcus probably had contacted a rescue team to get him off the mountain by now. It wouldn't be long before they faced a two-prong attack against those he loved.

His grandchildren and foster grandchild were in danger along with Freddie. Trying to protect them all in their various locations was too distracting. He needed a plan that would protect them all and also provide a way to stop the two men. He dialed Dianne again.

"Hey, what do you know about the ranch where Carlton Marsh is recuperating?"

"I know his sister, Tamera, operates the place as a therapy facility. She also teaches riding skills to youngsters. I went out there for a weekend and had a great time."

"I'm considering places to set a trap for Marcus and Alexander, but we don't need to endanger anyone else. Having a bunch of kids and therapy patients around probably wouldn't work. I'm also trying to find a safe place for my family and the witness."

"There's a remote retreat center on the property. Carlton's sister uses it on a rare occasion for an overnight camping trip. I stayed there once. The place is far away from her public riding areas and constructed with thick logs. That might work for a safe house."

Kent could hear Dianne's fingers tapping on her computer.

"It looks like there's a dirt road that isn't far from the cabin. You could move your family and *friend* in there for safekeeping, until you figure out how to set your trap."

Dianne's emphasis on the word friend, in reference to his witness, struck a chord in his heart. Yeah, Freddie was a friend for sure, maybe more if things worked out. He chose not to correct the secretary. "Good. Please arrange a flight for my son's family, Freddie, and me, out of Virginia. Notify the Hallmark family that I want to take Melissa on a trip for her own safety. We'll pick her up once we arrive. I'll need two cars at the airport. Assemble a crew of agents to surround the area for both protection and actively capturing the perpetrators when I set my trap. How is Carlton's recovery going?"

"Physically he's showing some improvement. Mentally he's beating himself up over allowing Jade Whitney's kidnapping from the ranch. Finding a full team of agents may be a challenge with Graham and his partner in the south and Carlton still trying to overcome his injuries."

"I'll see about asking if some of the Virginia agents can stay involved. Hold off on the flight arrangements until I see if they can come along." He'd enjoyed working with the younger agents. He doubted he could get the two injured agents reassigned, but Jared and Angela were forces to be reckoned with. They would prove valuable in a defensive operation.

"Hey, Dianne, I wonder if Jade's kidnapping might provide the lure to strike again in the same place, once we have agents in place. Call Agent Marsh and his sister to see if we can use their cabin, then send whoever you can find out there to set up a perimeter. We're coming back to Ohio, regardless. Let me know when you have things in place." Kent closed the conversation. Dianne was the best executive assistant. She'd have things done quickly and efficiently.

Smitty pulled the van close to what looked like the main entrance for the Roanoke office. "We've arrived at our headquarters. I've got orders to take Paul and Evan to the clinic. We'll drop the rest of you here."

Paul protested. Evan moaned in agreement.

Freddie said, "Thank you for going the extra mile to keep me from harm."

Kent noted the security guards just inside the glass double-door entrance. Good. He and Freddie could relax in safety until their flight to Ohio. He hurried out of the van. This time he would be the one to assist Freddie from the vehicle.

She stumbled while stepping out. He caught her arm and started leading her to the door. At first she pulled slightly away, then seemed to change her mind and leaned closer. Satisfaction, relief, and something more poured into his chest.

"I see where I rank." Angela's laughter followed them and broke into his train of thought.

"May I be of assistance, Miss Carpenter?" Agent Sutter's mocking voice made Kent and Freddie both look back over their linked arms to see Jared offer a gentlemanly elbow to assist Angela from the van. Both couples hurried into the protection of the federal building.

Jared led them to the office of the woman in charge. Agent Bea Whithers invited them to have seats in her utilitarian command center and offered coffee or tea. Kent noted that Freddie still preferred flavored teas. He chose a black coffee to boost his ebbing energy level. When the head agent offered homemade peanut butter cookies, he took a handful. They discussed the case between munching and sipping as energy flowed into his veins.

"As you can see, I could use another agent or two assigned to my dwindling team." Kent held up a cookie and laid a hand over his belly in a show of appreciation.

Bea laughed. "The way you keep losing team members doesn't give you a very good record. If I loan you my folks, are you going to return them in one piece?"

"I'll do my best. You know we can't promise the future. Only God can do that." Kent sobered. He didn't like losing people either.

Beside him, Freddie wrapped her arms tightly around her body.

~~~~~

"Are you cold, Miss Winifred?"

Freddie shook her head. "No. The last few days have been rough. I feel bad about causing everyone so much trouble."

Kent released a huff of air. "Trouble seems to follow you. I'm going to do all I can to bring this case to an end by solving the crime and ensuring my family's safety."

"Speaking of family, I usually try to connect with my dad and stepmom around this time of the month. Is there a computer I can use?" Freddie looked at the calendar on the wall behind Bea's desk as an ache to hug her father clenched in her chest. She'd missed that affection more than anything during the years of separation.

Bea and Kent frowned.

Kent took her hand. "Contacting them might put your parents in danger."

"What if they're already in danger or worried enough about me to draw attention to them?" She pulled away from his hand and gripped the sides of her chair. "Our contact is very minimal and just enough to let them know I'm not in trouble again. We use a coded email that has nothing to do with either of our real names. Please."

Kent turned to Bea. "What do you think?"

"I suggest that you observe, Agent Russell, and make sure nothing is given away in the message. We have a secure system for our internet. No one should be able to intercept it unless the parties have already given away their situations." The female agent's eyes seemed to pierce Freddie's soul.

Freddie squirmed in her seat like a guilty student. She looked down as her shoulders slumped. "I don't think we can be one hundred percent sure of anything these days. I did my best to hide. Kent's agents and Amber found me anyway, leaving a trail for Marcus and Alexander to follow. I figure it won't be long until Winnie Gee's hidden name is out for
~~~~~

the entire world to see."

Bea's eyebrows rose. "Are you saying that you know Winnie Gee? My daughter buys her books for the preschoolers she teaches."

"She not only knows Winnie Gee, she's one and the same. I'm planning on an autograph session with my grandsons after this case is over." Pride rang in Kent's pronouncement.

Bea smiled. "I hope you'll invite my family too."

"So, does that mean I can contact my publisher after I message Dad and Lindy?" Freddie grinned at her two fans. She didn't normally take advantage of Winnie's fame, but making an exception seemed like a good idea. She needed a distraction from the threats and danger thrown at her over the last few days. Besides, the publisher needed to know there might be a delay on the completion of her next project.

"As long as Agent Russell is satisfied with your communication, feel free to use Paul's computer. The door to his office is the third one to your left. His desk is by the window." Bea waved them out of the room as she picked up a stack of paperwork.

For the first time in several days, a sense of independence washed over Freddie. She straightened her shoulders and marched down the hall to the indicated office. Jared and Angela sat at two of the four desks. They nodded but kept inputting information into their computers. Freddie wondered if they were writing up reports about their adventures in the mountains. She headed for the desk by the window. She sat and wiggled the mouse. Nothing happened. Kent followed and pulled an extra chair up behind her.

Angela joined them. "Let me put in my password so you can open the computer. You can use it as needed after it wakes up."

Freddie waited until all the pings of applications starting up cleared. She opened her Winnie Gee email account and typed a message to her publisher. "I have some personal conflicts during the next few weeks. Can we delay the publication of my next book accordingly?" She signed off as Winnie Gee and pointed to the screen.

Kent leaned close to inspect the message. His breath and a wisp of hair warmed her neck.

"That looks fine." Kent lingered near her shoulder. His hands rested on either side of her chair.

Her hand shook as she tried to concentrate on opening another window for the server used to message Dad. She closed her eyes and offered a short prayer. *Help me deal with these renewed feelings for Kent. Please keep my family safe. I pray in Jesus' name, Amen.*

"Are you okay?" His whisper in her ear warmed her whole body.

"I'm doing great." She leaned back into his chest. They both sighed as she typed in her message.

Hi Dad and Lindy. Just checking in. Be careful. Hugs, W.G.

Kent nodded his approval, and she hit send. She didn't normally sign off with "hugs," but she wanted to convey how much she missed Dad. Since she had no siblings or children, he was her only family. She didn't even have any stepsiblings since her stepmom, Lindy, married for the first time when she met Dad later in life.

Warm hands moved to her shoulders, reminding her of what could have been and what might be in her future. She reached up and linked her fingers with his as they waited for responses. It didn't take long for her publisher to reply with permission to proceed once the conflicts cleared up. Asking for a delay was a first for Freddie, so the publisher must have understood that her reasons for the request were important and excusable.

When a half hour passed with no answer from her dad, Freddie's knee jiggled. She picked up a pen and started drawing random characters from different angles on a nearby pad of paper. Why weren't they answering? Dad always sent at least a confirmation within a few minutes. The only time he hadn't answered right away was when he broke an arm. Lindy sent a message within fifteen minutes on that day.

Chapter Sixteen

Kent finished texting his son about the latest change of plans as he watched Freddie grow more agitated. "I take it your dad or stepmom usually answer right away."

"True. I don't recall ever waiting this long for an email response. I'm getting worried. Is there anything you can do, maybe have someone do a wellness check?" She stood and paced around the small office. Angela rose and stopped her with a hug.

Kent shook his head. He should have offered to take her in his arms. He was rusty at comforting women. He'd messed that one up. Taking charge of the case was more his expertise. He pulled out his phone and called Dianne. "I need someone out west to check on Miss Grimsley's parents. I don't care if it's our agency or local law enforcement, but someone needs to locate them pronto."

"Give me an address, and I'll take care of it."

"Hold on." He asked Freddie for the information and then relayed her parents' Arizona address to Dianne.

After hanging up, he did what he should have done in the first place. Pulling Freddie close to his chest, he held her tightly. Warm moisture seeped into his shirt from her silent tears. She'd been a trouper so far, even conquering her fear of heights back on the mountain. He rested his chin on the top of her head and closed his eyes. Visions of happy times from long ago swam across his mind until his phone rang again. He gave her one more comforting squeeze before stepping away to answer the call from his son.

"Hey, Dad. I got your message. Chelsea and the kids will meet you at the Roanoke office in about an hour. I can't get the time off from work, but the boss is sending me on a business trip out of the country for the next week. I should be safe enough since there is high security involved."

"Just be careful, son."

Kent prayed for his son's safety. He couldn't wait to see the rest of the family and introduce them to their favorite writer and illustrator, Winnie Gee. He moved closer to where Freddie had settled next to Angela. Their voices were low, but he caught bits and pieces of their conversation about her parents. He pulled a chair over and laid an arm across Freddie's shoulders.

"After my mother passed away, Dad stayed single for a while. Lindy knew my parents and gradually grew to be more than a family friend. She supplied what he needed, but I still miss Mom." Freddie lifted a tissue to her nose.

Kent rubbed Freddie's back. "Your dad and I were good friends during his roughest days. Neither one of us was sure what to do when you disappeared. Then he disappeared too. I didn't know what to do other than assume neither of you wanted my friendship anymore."

"I cut off ties for your own safety. At the time, I didn't feel like I had any other choice. If only I'd been a braver woman in the past." Freddie lowered her head.

"You've proven your strength throughout this trip." Angela gave Freddie's hand a pat. "I suggest both of you move on to the future." The female agent wiggled her eyebrows as she gave Kent a knowing look.

"I'm hoping my future will include Freddie." He glanced at her. A slight smile crossed Freddie's face, making his heart rate increase. For now, they had to survive the next few days and whatever the trial for MAX Enterprises employees brought their way.

The chatter of youthful voices echoed in the hallway. Kent smiled. "I believe my grandchildren and daughter-in-law, Chelsea, have arrived." Bea led Chelsea and two excited boys into the room. He held his arms wide. The two youngsters scampered across the room and into his lap.

"Grandpa, we've been camping for the last week. Mom cooked canned food most of the time. It wasn't too good, so I ordered a pizza." His older grandson, Mason, frowned.

"Daddy got grumpy after Mason called the pizza man," Jordan, Kent's younger grandson, tattled.

"He said I broke your camping rules. I'm sorry I messed up, but can you maybe make pizza one of the food rules next time?" Mason's sorrowful eyes put a begging Basset hound to shame.

Kent bounced a grandson on each knee. "Our next stop will be a horse ranch."

"Are we going to get a pizza at the horse ranch?" Mason rubbed his tummy.

"I rode a pony at the fair last year." Jordan bounced on Grandpa's other knee.

"I hope you both can ride and have pizza, but obeying my rules is going to be very important while we're there. Do you promise to be good?"

Both boys nodded and then wrapped their arms around Kent's neck.

Chelsea cleared her throat. "I'm glad you promised, boys. Let's make sure we don't break the rules this time." She stood between two large rolling suitcases and shifted to look at each of her sons in turn.

When she faced Kent, he saw weariness showing in new lines around her eyes.

"I'm sorry to put you all through this, but you know the reasons." He left the details out as he glanced at the boys. "Are you ready to take an airplane ride?"

"Will it be a little plane like Frieda Flyer?" Jordan referred to the title characters of one of Winnie Gee's latest picture books.

"Our jet will be a smaller one, but not as little as Frieda. Miss Freddie might have something special to share with you about your storybook plane. She knows everything about the person who created Frieda."

"Does she know Winnie Gee?"

"Something like that. We can talk later on the plane or at the ranch." Freddie squinted and gave a slight head shake.

Kent got the message. Too many eyes and ears in the office and she wasn't ready to do a big reveal yet. He'd already let her author status out of the bag with Bea. Had he overstepped?

~~~~~

Freddie looked away when Kent's phone rang. He stepped into the hall. She smiled at the two young boys' questioning faces. Kent's grandsons were adorable, much like their grandfather when he wasn't trying to tell the world all her secrets.

Maybe he was right. She'd held too many things away from others since leaving Max's employ. Back in Lee County she only had two close friends. Mary, who had steered her back to a loving relationship with God, and Rick, who provided a father figure in the absence of her own parents.

Why hadn't Dad or Lindy responded? She pushed those worries to the back of her mind. Freddie needed to do right by the children in front of her. She bent down and opened her arms to the boys, who looked up at their mother for confirmation. The younger woman nodded and they edged closer.

"I am going to tell you something that not too many people know. Do you think you would like to be one of Winnie Gee's special friends?"

The boys nodded.

"Your grandfather tells me you like Winnie Gee stories. He just found out I write and illustrate those books. He wanted me to share that with you."

"I thought your name was Freddie. That's a weird name for a girl. One of my friends in preschool was named Freddy." The youngster's concentration seemed to wander for a moment. Freddie drew him closer.

"My real name is Winifred Grimsley. When I was your age, some people shortened my name to Winnie. I decided to use that part of my name for my writing, along with the first initial of my last name, G. I really am Winnie Gee."

"I like that better than Freddie. Can we call you Winnie?" Jordan wiggled like a delighted puppy. Mason's face held an expression of awe
~~~~~

as his mouth dropped open.

"We should call her Miss Freddie until this adventure is over, don't you agree, ma'am?" Their mother intervened before Freddie had a chance to speak.

"Yes, I agree, and hope you will use my first name too. I could use some friends."

"I will be your friend." Mason had found his voice.

"Me too." Jordan gave her a hug. Mason joined his brother until they both stepped back to their mother in what looked like a bout of shyness.

Chelsea Russell's shoulders lowered. She reached out and the two women clasped hands. "I'm glad to meet you. I just wish it was under different circumstances. I've been in constant prayer over this whole situation."

"My prayer has been for forgiveness. Too many people are in danger because of my choices. Your family shouldn't have to endure this and neither should my dad and stepmom. I'm so sorry." Freddie gave Chelsea's hands a squeeze and then released them.

"At least the boys and I will get to visit our former foster child. They're looking forward to reuniting with Melissa after a year apart. We've messaged back and forth, but we all miss her. These guys really liked living in Ohio. It's been an adjustment for the whole family, but Lachlan couldn't afford to turn down the promotion. I hated giving up caring for Melissa, but a wonderful family adopted her." Chelsea looked down when Mason tugged on her shirt hem. He waved her to his level and whispered something in his mom's ear.

The young mother pulled a couple of drawing pads and boxes of colored pencils from her oversized purse and directed the children to an empty desk. "If it is okay with you, the boys would like to show you their drawings your books inspired."

Within moments, the two boys had flipped through previously done plane drawings and were sketching new ones that resembled young attempts at Frieda the Flyer. Chelsea motioned for Freddie to join her near the door.

"Will your parents meet us at the ranch?"

"I'm not sure. We tried to contact them earlier today and they haven't answered. Dad or my stepmother, Lindy, usually answers within minutes." Freddie angled so she could see Kent farther down the hall. He had his back to them. She couldn't make out what he said. "I hoped his call was about them."

Chelsea grinned like a Cheshire cat. "What I want to know is why my father-in-law looks like he wants to hold you in his arms."

"Unfortunately, he knows me better than most. We dated a long time ago, until I disappeared to get away from a bad situation. I thought I protected him by running. Now, my mistakes are catching up and causing the present, uh, situation." She'd started to say danger, but curbed her words so the children wouldn't worry.

"I have no doubt that Grandpa Kent will guard us with his life. I'm willing to assume he would do the same for you. How about sitting down with Mason and Jordan? You can give them some drawing lessons. That might be a good distraction for all."

The feel of working with pencil and paper awoke Freddie's creative gifts. As she doodled with Chelsea and the boys, she prayed for Dad, Lindy, Kent, and his family. Her thoughts zoomed back to the days when she'd taught Max's young Amber a few art skills. They'd drawn with pencils and paper too. Gluing transistors and diodes onto paper in special designs had fascinated Amber.

One day they'd found a diode with the numbers 1N1776 printed on the side. Max had walked in while Freddie had shared that 1776 was an important year. He'd asked for the diode and kept it on his desk in a container full of paper clips. She wondered how she'd even remembered the event. Then she recalled Amber asking her daddy to tell her more. The man had flipped the diode in the air, caught it, and told the girl he was busy.

"Miss Freddie can handle the history lesson once she gets her work done." He'd gone into his office grinning as he studied the small electronic piece.

Tears ran down young Amber's face that day, but she hadn't let out a whimper. Freddie recalled attempting to type for a minute before abandoning her work and wrapping her arms around the young girl. They'd become friends and supporters of each other after that historic day.

Could the numbers on the diode be part of the code that Alexander and Marcus sought? Max had seemed obsessed with the little gadget, fingering it as he gave daily work assignments for her to complete. Freddie sketched the diode on her paper.

"Is that a jellyfish floating in the sky?" Jordan asked.

Freddie laughed. "I suppose it could be. We should draw some flying fish coming to visit Frieda and the jellyfish."

"Maybe we should have some seahorses for them to ride when they go to the ranch." Mason's admiring expression met Freddie's gaze.

"That sounds like a fine idea. Are you ready to fly to the ranch?" Kent stood in the doorway, his expression guarded.

Chapter Seventeen

After spending the night at secure housing near the Roanoke office, Kent knocked on doors of his family and crew for an early wake-up call. Angela would accompany them to Ohio and had spent the night in a room with Freddie. Bea Withers also agreed to loan Jared for protection duty for the time being. Kent had shared hall duty with the male agent during the night hours. Once everyone was ready to move, they went to the airport tarmac in vehicles with dark windows.

Loneliness enveloped Kent as he followed the group headed into the small jet provided by the Federal agency. The night before, when Freddie confessed to having a fear of heights to his grandchildren, the boys had assured her they would provide safety by sitting on either side of her. Kent had pointed out that their jet had two seats on one side of the aisle and another across the way. The boys made their plan by suggesting one of them would sit next to her while the other sat across the aisle. They'd let Grandpa know they didn't want anything to happen to their Winnie Gee now that she was their friend. As planned, Freddie currently sat in the aisle seat surrounded by her young fans. Chelsea had taken the single seat behind them.

The pair of Virginia agents found seats behind the clustered group. They waved him back, probably to talk about a plan. That was where his mind should be, but his thoughts drifted to his loved ones ahead as he claimed the single seat near his fellow workers. Instead of immediately addressing the case, Kent's grandchildren drew his attention.

Mason leaned his elbows on the armrest and glared at his brother, who'd claimed the seat next to Freddie. In the exchange, Jordan leaned over Freddie and stuck his tongue out as he wiggled fingers near his ears.

Freddie shook her head. "You both should make better choices than exchanging mean faces. You might end up inspiring a grumpy character in one of my next books. I'd rather have you in a story about someone who is happy."

"Sorry," both boys chimed in together.

"Would you really put us in one of your books?" Mason's eyes grew big.

"I will, if you two promise to behave like one of my good characters."

Jordan and Mason nodded as they bounced in their seats.

Freddie reached across the aisle and shook hands with Mason and then turned toward Jordan. The three of them laid hands on top of each other, sealing a pact to be nice. Chelsea stuck her head into the aisle and whispered something that made the boys nod and Freddie smile.

The pilot indicated seatbelt use and everyone settled in place for their flight. As they taxied toward take-off, Kent noted the boys had once again reached out to Freddie. They were holding her hands and telling her to close her eyes so she wouldn't be afraid.

"Riding a plane is fun. Pretend Frieda the Flyer is taking you on a trip," Jordan advised.

"Frieda won't let you down. You have to tell her no loops this time," Mason added.

Freddie laughed. "I will ask her to not loop."

Warmth spread across Kent's chest as he watched the bond grow between Freddie and his family. The lift in his chest came from more than the airplane leaving the ground. She'd make a wonderful grandparent if things worked out. First, they had to lay a trap for Alexander and Marcus. Feeling like someone watched him, he turned to look at Angela.

She had a knowing smile on her face. "She's an admirable woman. Are you thinking beyond this case?"

"Maybe. Nothing is promised. We need to figure out a way to lead the criminals to our location without bringing any harm to my family or hers. I still haven't heard back from Freddie's parents. They've got to be in their mid-seventies or older. She's hiding her reactions well, but I imagine their lack of communication is bothering her."

"Did you hear anything back from law enforcement near her parents' location?" Jared asked.

"They found no one at home. The place didn't look disturbed. A neighbor said Mr. and Mrs. Grimsley asked him to water their flowerbeds until they got home. I'm hoping they are on a vacation in a remote area, but not giving the neighbor an end date doesn't feel right to me."

"Speaking of remote places, tell us a little about this place we're headed and why you think it will provide both safety and a way to arrest the criminals." Angela grabbed her armrest as the plane bumped through a cloud.

Squeals from Freddie and the children gave Kent a moment to formulate his reply. "Carlton, an injured agent on my team, is currently recuperating on his sister's equine therapy ranch in western Ohio. The place is rural and mostly flat land. My secretary assures me that there is a remote area on the property surrounded by woods. That site has a small retreat center where we can house everyone and protect them all at once.

"There's a county road that runs on the north side of the place, serving as a dividing line between two properties. The owner of the other land has it mostly surrounded by a high fence. The enclosure should keep them from coming at us from the other property's direction. I'm going to arrange for several RVs to park there and let it leak that we'll be staying in them. I'm hoping Alexander and Marcus will go to those vehicles and we can surround them."

"Will we drive directly to this ranch after we land?" Angela asked.

"No. We have one more family member under threat. We'll stop by my regional office to pick up my former foster granddaughter, Melissa. Her adoptive parents will bring her there. The child will think she is going on vacation with the family that fostered her. I'd like to keep it that way if possible."

"Understood. Will her new family go with us?" The plane leveled out. Jared leaned across the aisle.

"No. They've decided to stay away. Their youngest children might be more of a distraction than a help. Our enemies don't see me as having an attachment to them so they should be safe. Melissa's new parents, Ginny and Scott, are taking their little ones to his mother's out-of-town home for the next couple of weeks as an added measure of security. Once everything is set in place, we will ask them to put a message on social media, letting the world know about Melissa taking an RV camping trip with my family on the back property of a certain friend's horse therapy ranch. The criminals will know where to search because the property is the scene of one of their earlier crimes."

~~~~~

Freddie's stomach dropped as the plane bounced several times along the Toledo runway. Kent's grandsons each held one of her hands, reminding her to contain her fears as the jet rushed to a swift halt before taxiing toward the small terminal. Many years had passed since she'd seen the place. One private jet sat on the tarmac. No commercial planes lined up nearby. The last time she'd flown from the airport was before her fear of heights became part of her life, before her European education, and before her life as a teacher. She'd run away to save her boyfriend from harm and provide herself with an unknown future away from MAX Enterprises. A warm trail of moisture made its way down her cheek.

"Don't cry, Miss Freddie. We landed just fine." Mason leaned closer.

"Frieda would be proud of our pilot." Jordan patted her arm

"You are right." Freddie gave each boy's hand a squeeze and swiped away the tears from her face. Reaching down, she started to unbuckle her seatbelt.

"Stop. You can't take your seatbelt off until the light says you can." Jordan pointed to the instruction light above their heads. "You have to follow the rules or you'll get in trouble."

Kent cleared his throat from a few seats back. "You boys need to remember the rules when we get to the horse ranch."
~~~~~

"Mason ordered pizza, not me. I was good," Jordan said

"You didn't mind taking the pizza man's free token for another pizza." Mason crossed his arms and wiggled sideways in his seat with the belt still holding him somewhat in place.

"At least I didn't lose mine. I've still got it in my backpack." Jordan smirked.

Sensing a potential war of words, Freddie leaned between the two children and pointed to the lone private jet. "If I put a plane like that one in a Frieda story, what would be a good name? I'm going to need at least ten choices. Then we will each have three votes to use on our top choices."

For several moments the boys and Freddie brainstormed ideas. She was impressed with their list.

"I like Georgie the Jet," Mason said.

"Me, too, but what if the jet is another girl, like Frieda?" Jordan tugged on Freddie's arm.

"Georgie might work as a girl's name too. Freddie works for Winifred." Kent spoke from behind them.

"Then I will call the jet, Georgie." Freddie smiled at the two boys.

Jordan high-fived his brother as a ping sounded, calling attention to the seatbelt sign blinking off.

Freddie stood and looked back at Kent. Lowered eyebrows cut across his features as he edged down the aisle. What was wrong with him this time?

Kent stopped near Jordan and asked to see the pizza token.

The boy fished inside his bag and pulled out a coin-shaped piece of metal with an M embossed on one side. "Here you go, Grandpa. The man said I could get a free pizza if I kept this with me."

Freddie watched as Kent separated the coin-shaped piece into two halves, revealing a flat compartment holding a small electronic device. He dropped the blinking gadget onto the floor and crushed it with his heel.

"I'll get your next pizza, Jordan. That man was lying to you both." He gave the whimpering boy a hug and started leading his grandchild down the aisle as he flung the superhero backpack over one shoulder. "Everyone needs to gather their things quickly and get out of here. I'm afraid the pizza delivery guy has tricked all of us with a tracker."

As they hurried down the deplaning stairs connected to their plane, another jet began its descent to the ground. MAX Enterprises lettering covered the tailfin. Their followers weren't far behind.

Freddie prayed for their safety as she and the others ran for the waiting government vehicles Kent had pointed them toward. Jared and Angela directed Chelsea and the boys into the larger SUV. Kent wrapped his arm around Freddie until they climbed into the back seat of the other car. Movement near the terminal caught her eye.

A rough-looking man dressed in a chauffeur's outfit glanced their way as he spoke on a cell phone. He turned his focus to the MAX Enterprises plane taxiing closer and threw a hand in the air. Kent pushed her lower in the seat and gave the word to move out using two different routes to headquarters.

"With children involved, this isn't the time to confront the lone driver. Let's put some distance between us and the occupants of the arriving plane."

Sorrow for all that was happening rolled over Freddie as the cars sped away. If only she could turn back time and make a different decision. Kent's hand rested on her lowered shoulders, but she didn't deserve his concern. In running away to save him as a young man, she'd only brought trouble on his family in the present. He'd indicated a renewed interest, but could anything develop between them when she might possibly be a witness that would need to go into hiding? Or was she an accomplice to a crime based on the fact she'd chosen to hide the truth from law enforcement in the past? Only God could help her out of this jam she'd made by her own doing.

Chapter Eighteen

Kent directed the driver to head straight to the horse ranch. He called Chelsea and had her give the phone to Jared. "Have your driver head to the retreat, but take an indirect route. We'll do the same."

"We had the same idea. I'll reconfirm with the driver. Here's Chelsea." Jared's muffled voice shared the order.

"What about Melissa?" Chelsea's voice shook.

"I'll contact Dianne and have another agent take her to our safe house at the ranch. Don't worry. Everyone will be fine." At least he hoped that was the case. The situation became more complicated by the minute. He'd asked the Hallmarks to bring the girl to his office. He prayed she was safely there already.

Dianne answered the phone on the first ring. "What's your status, Boss? We have a darling young lady waiting here to see your family."

"Tell her we've had a slight change of plans. Get a trusted agent to drive her out to where Carlton is staying. Make that a couple of agents. They need to be alert to followers. We had a welcoming committee at the airport. It won't be long before they are on our tail."

"Will do, Boss. By the way, we are a man down. Our mole, Martin, shot Graham during a takedown. Martin is in custody and a little worse for wear thanks to Amber, Landon, and some fire ants. Graham is recovering in the hospital from his injuries. He should be released within a week. Landon is driving home from Alabama as we speak."

"Good. Send him to the ranch once he arrives. Did they make any progress with solving the clues Max left behind?"

"Using a homemade radio, Amber was able to hear her father's recorded message. It looks like the old man came clean. We have the names of the whole cybercriminal ring, including Marcus and Alexander as major players, beneath their leader, Victoria. Maybe those two will give up the chase when they hear the news."

"I'm not so sure. They seem to think Miss Grimsley knows a code that will lead them to something important. I have no proof, but I would guess an offshore bank account or a device that will make money on the black market so they can afford to disappear." He'd chosen to use Freddie's proper address to avoid Dianne's inquiries about their relationship.

"Has *your* Miss Freddie thought of what the code might be?"

So much for distracting his secretary... "I know Freddie's given it some thought, but she has no idea about how to try anything out. Our goal at this time is to apprehend the two men without harming any civilians. Then we can look for any other surprises Max left for us."

"Speaking of surprises, Melissa is peering in my doorway. Would you like to speak with her?"

"Of course." He wouldn't pass up an opportunity to speak with the sweet child that he still considered a grandchild.

"Hi, Grandpa Russell, I'm so excited to see everyone again. Is it true that we might get to ride a horse?" Her voice seemed to bubble with expectation.

"Hey, sweetheart, I hope we can work that out. We've had a slight change of plans. Instead of meeting you at my office, I'm going to have my agents take you to the ranch. I want you to be really good for them on the way there. Pretend you're on a secret mission and keep your head low so no one can see you. Can you promise to do that?"

"I can. Mom and Dad said something about watching out for bad guys. I guess this is part of staying away from them."

Kent ground his teeth together. So much for keeping the child in the dark... "That's true, but we don't want to say anything to upset the boys. They think we're on an adventure. They aren't as old as you are."

"Don't worry, Grandpa. I'll help make the trip an adventure for them. I know how to keep secrets from everyone except Mom and Dad. That all changed when they adopted me."

Kent knew the girl's history all too well. Living with a negligent mother for the first part of her life had given Melissa a different perspective about surviving in difficult situations. "You're a brave one. I love you and look forward to seeing you at the ranch."

"I love you, too, Grandpa. Miss Dianne wants to talk to you. Bye."

After two feminine voices faded into the background, his secretary answered using quiet tones. "I've shooed her out of the room. Do you still think it's wise to move her out to the ranch? I'm wondering if she wouldn't be safer here."

Kent relayed his plans for parking the recreational vehicles on the back of the property as a decoy and asked Dianne to locate available camping trailers. "I want her safe with the rest of the family at the retreat center. We need every available agent you can send my way to be either in those RVs or surrounding my loved ones. See if you can recruit people from either Michigan or Indiana if you have to. This is too personal when they threaten my family."

Freddie's restless fingers in her lap reminded him about her dad and stepmom. "Have we gotten any more information on Mr. and Mrs. Grimsley?"

"There's nothing new. I promise to let you know as soon as I know something." Dianne confirmed his thoughts in a crisp voice. He'd asked the question for Freddie's sake, not his own. He shook his head so she'd know and signed off with Dianne.

"Could I try calling them?" Freddie's eyes pled with him. He handed her his phone and watched her place the call. Her fingers shook as she tapped in the numbers.

"Put it on speaker. It has been too long since I heard your dad's voice."

The phone rang several times before a young voice answered. "Hello?"

"Who is this, and why do you have my dad's phone?" Freddie gripped the phone closer as she faced Kent with a panicked expression.

"I'm Jimmy. My friends and I were out walking and heard the phone ringing under this bush. I don't know who it belongs to. I just picked it up."

~~~~~

Freddie's breath caught in her throat. She held the device in a tightened fist between Kent and her. Had Alexander or Marcus found Dad and Lindy? Her ears rang from the pressure building up inside, muffling Kent's reply to Jimmy. She had to get in control and not panic. Forcing her breathing to regulate, she concentrated on the continuing conversation until she could understand their words.

"Listen carefully, Jimmy. After we hang up, I want you to lay the phone down where you found it. I'm going to contact local law enforcement to come to the location you gave me. Can you do that for me?" Kent wrapped his fingers around hers. She loosened her grip that had started to cramp.

"I can do that, sir. This is cool. It's like a regular law enforcement show." Other youthful voices chattered in the background.

"Well, Jimmy, this time you are going to be part of the real thing. I need you and your buddies to stay put and tell the policemen all about where you found the phone. With your parents' permission, the police may want a copy of your fingerprints since you touched the device. Do you or one of your friends have a way to call your parents? We don't want them worrying if this takes a while."

"Yes, sir, we all have phones. Hey, guys, let your parents know we're here." His enthusiasm increased in volume as he called out to his friends. Freddie was tempted to plug her ears, but didn't want to miss any more of the conversation than she had already.

After Kent's final instructions to the boy, Freddie released the phone to Kent, who gave her arm a reassuring squeeze. She stared as he tapped the cell and started the process of connecting with the Arizona authorities.

Dad always answered her calls. Finding the cell discarded in a bush wasn't what she'd hoped for when dialing him minutes ago. Her world
~~~~~

had gone from routine to dangerous in a matter of days that felt like an eternity. Behind her lay a trail of people who were facing harm because of her actions. Her parents, Rick, school children, the family no longer having the use of their farmhouse, two federal agents, Kent's family, and the boys waiting for law enforcement out west, were all in some degree of danger.

Amber and her federal agents had found answers, but were they truly safe? Now Alexander and Marcus were doing their best to capture Freddie for a code she hadn't known existed before her week started. If they did manage to get to her, she wouldn't know what answer to give them. A part of her being wanted to cave in and end the whole thing, but only a small part. She was strong and smart. Her choices hadn't always been the best, but she'd survived. Overcoming situations had become part of who she was, and going forward was all she knew how to do. Somehow, she would get through this with God's help.

City buildings gave way to trees and flat open fields as the driver of their SUV headed toward the less populated areas. The flat land was a deep contrast to the mountains of Lee County, Virginia. An occasional cow came into view as they passed red and white barns and waving fields of wheat. Her eyes drifted closed. Her mind flip-flopped between prayers and slumber. *Dear Lord, help us all get to this ranch without harm.* Peace enveloped her as sleep overtook her tired body.

Their vehicle's sudden acceleration pushed her back against the seat, putting her confidence-building self-talk and prayers to the test. There was only one reason for the driver to be accelerating. They'd only seen one chauffer at the airport. At least the criminals behind them had followed their car and not the driver delivering family members to the ranch. Her faith wavered for only a second before she returned to petitioning God. *Please Lord, if You can't keep us from harm, at least spare the children.*

An impact sent the SUV spinning. Freddie grabbed the armrest and seat beneath her, preparing for what might happen next. A glimpse at their driver's profile showed him concentrating on what he was doing. If she wasn't mistaken, the man looked like he was in control and ready to take on the world.

As they came out of the spin, he shouted, "Brace yourselves, I'm going on the offense."

Another crash shook their vehicle, but they kept going. The criminals' car spun out of control and landed on its side in the deep ditch that ran parallel to the road.

"Do you want me to stop or keep heading for our destination, Boss?" the driver asked in a steady voice.

"Keep going, Victor. I'll phone it in to the locals. I want to catch them, but right now the safety of our witness is more important." Kent took a look behind them before lifting his phone to make the call.

Freddie grabbed his arm before he had a chance to dial. "Wouldn't it be better to catch them now?"

"This time I'm the one making the decision to run, not you. We know who they are. There's enough processed evidence in our hands right now to put those two behind bars. I'm not taking a chance on them coming out of that car ready to shoot at us and capture you."

"I'm tired of running." Freddie wanted to stop the car and put this all behind her.

"I know, but if they have your parents, they might convince you to surrender because of worry or guilt over their capture. We also need time for you to come up with some possible codes or fake codes."

He knew her all too well. Saving her Dad and Lindy was forefront in her thoughts. Looking away, she closed her eyes and thought back on the possible codes that had come to mind.

"I might have some ideas. Whether my ideas are real or fake, I have no way of confirming."

"I know." Kent dialed 9-1-1 and spoke to the dispatcher about the car in the ditch.

The trees and fields flew faster past her window as the driver made a few more turns and sped forward in a westward direction. The setting sun burned into her eyes, forcing them to close as she hardened her heart. Kent was right about one thing. If the chance arose to save everyone, including him, she'd put her life on the line. She'd done the wrong thing in the past by running. Now was the future. The time would come when she might be forced to take a stand.

Chapter Nineteen

Kent dialed Chelsea and asked her to give her phone to Jared. "Tell your driver to be ready for evasion. We just took a hit and left the attacker in a ditch for local law enforcement to clean up. I have no idea how many hired people they have working for them now that we are in home territory."

"Got it, Boss. Here's Chelsea." Kent heard Jared share the information in the background as Chelsea's wavering voice came through the cell.

"Are you and Miss Freddie free from harm?" Concern laced her voice.

"We're a little shaken, but we're in one piece. Take care of my grandsons."

"You know I will. They're looking forward to riding a horse with Miss Freddie and Grandpa." Her voice sounded stronger. Good for her. She needed to set a positive example for the boys.

"We'll see you all soon." Kent signed off and leaned forward to speak with the driver.

"Victor, instead of going to the retreat center, I'd like to head to the ranch headquarters where Agent Carlton is recuperating. I'm going to need all the help I can get, and I need to know his current capabilities and any insight he can give about the lay of the land."

"Sure thing, Boss." Victor steered the car onto a side road. As he barreled ahead, the man cleared his throat. "I heard through the grapevine that Carlton's last physical check-up went well. Guilty feelings about Jade's kidnapping are eating at him though."

"He's a good agent. I'm sorry that the situation is affecting him. Maybe our actions in the next few days will counterbalance his concerns about his abilities." Kent leaned back next to Freddie. "Any idea when we'll reach our destination?"

"If we don't have any more run-ins with troublemakers, we should be there in about half an hour using the most direct route." Victor scanned the mirrors and focused on the road ahead.

"Go for it. The sooner we get there, the better I'll feel about everyone's safety." Kent glanced over at Freddie. She had closed eyes, but she sat stiff and upright. Movement in her jaw implied tension. Was she thinking of fleeing again? He hoped not. A runaway witness was the last thing his case or heart needed. He reached over and took one of her fisted hands.

"Relax, Freddie. You can trust me to help you this time. Look at me and promise you won't do anything stupid."

She didn't open her eyes. A frown creased her forehead. Her clenched hand remained closed.

"That's what I was afraid of." Stubborn woman. He could be stubborn too. He kept his hand on hers and massaged her knuckles with his thumb.

Thoughts of the future danced across his mind like swirling leaves in the fall. If only she'd trusted him enough to share her troubles in the past. He brushed those thoughts aside. Love for his son, daughter-in-law, and grandchildren were his present blessings. Wishing for something that never happened was useless. Praying for patience, he dared to close his eyes for a few moments.

The car lurched to a stop. "We're at the ranch, sir." Victor's voice woke Kent.

Freddie's hand had relaxed into his. It looked like they'd both had a nap. She lifted her hand from his to cover a yawn. He watched the driver stride around the car and hold the door open for her. She stood without a word and seemed to be surveying the place. A horse whinnied from the corral next to a red barn. A hint of a smile crossed her face and then vanished when the door to the ranch house opened.

"Come on in, Boss. You look like you've been through the wringer since the last time I saw you." Carlton waved from the porch.

"I could say the same about you, Carlton." Kent gave his agent a clap on the back, careful to not get in the way of the man's cane.

"I've graduated to a walking stick. Give me another few days and I'll be ready to run a marathon." Carlton's grin didn't quite match his sorrowful eyes.

Kent wanted to know more about what was going on inside his agent's head. "I have doubts about your running skills at the moment, but would you be willing to stand guard with a gun if we need you?"

Carlton's gaze met Kent's, his voice full of defeat. "I'd be glad to help any way I can. Guilt has been eating me alive since the kidnapping."

"Jade has been found. You should let that burden go. Right now, I'd like to pick your brain about the ranch and this retreat center. We need to put our plan in place as soon as possible."

Carlton opened the door and led them into the home. "Come on in. My older sister, Tamera, has been running the place since my foster parents retired to Florida. It used to be a foster home for troubled kids like me. After I discovered I had an older sister, they took her in as an employee to help finish my raising. She stayed on after I entered agent training and changed everything to a horse therapy ranch when the parents retired."

Freddie stepped into a half bathroom while Kent followed his agent farther into the house. Tamera met them with a Geological Survey map and a fresh pot of coffee.

"There's a lot of acreage between here and the retreat center." She flattened the one-mile-square map on a large wooden table. "The road that runs closest to the retreat center consists of a neglected gravel trail that I've not used much in the last few years. If your team comes in using RVs, you may want Carlton to run the bush hog through the area."

"I can definitely handle the big mower," Carlton volunteered.

"Good." Kent acknowledged Carlton's willingness with a nod as Freddie joined them.

"Our neighbor put a fence up along that lane during the last few years to ensure her rescued mules stay on her property. She's a private person. I don't have much contact with her, so I doubt she'll even see what's going on due to several acres of trees on this end of her property, though she might hear shooting if things don't go down quietly. She wasn't real happy about the Fourth of July firecrackers we set off last summer because they spooked some of her mules. I'll be taking care of my own horses during this scheme of yours. I've cancelled therapy for this week. I told everyone I needed a vacation with my brother."

"This won't be a fun time for anyone. I'm sorry to cause trouble for everyone." Freddie broke her silence with her apology.

"Catching these crooks will make everyone feel better. Your testimony is an important factor. Don't worry about what happened in the past. We only have the future." Kent picked up the map. "Let's roll with the plan. How soon can we get the road bush hogged so the RVs can move in?"

"I'll head to the barn now, and get the mower hooked to our tractor." Carlton limped out the backdoor while his sister escorted Kent and Freddie to the front porch.

"I pray everything goes according to plan. Carlton and I feel really bad about what happened to Jade. I'm glad she's safe now." Tamera leaned against the doorframe.

"Take care of yourself and know that both of you are forgiven. We appreciate the use of your retreat center and back road. If you see any problems here, don't be afraid to contact 9-1-1 or my secretary, Dianne. She will know where we're at with the operation. I assume you have her number since you seem to be friends."

"I do. My prayers are with you." Tamera turned and went inside, closing the door behind her.

As they walked toward their waiting car, Kent's phone rang. He took one look at his screen and answered Dianne's call.

"Hey, Boss. I've got some information on Freddie's parents and you're not going to like it."

~~~~~
~~~~~

As a teacher, Freddie had learned to read people's emotions. She watched Kent's expression go from solemn to angry. Whatever he heard wasn't good news. She prayed it wasn't about his family or hers, but knew the chances were good that his conversation involved one or the other. He turned and stalked away, pacing back and forth until he shoved the phone into his pocket.

The concerned look on his face didn't bode well as he approached her and reached for her hands. She swallowed, preparing for the worst. "Is it my parents?"

"The local law enforcement processed the scene near where the boys found your dad's phone. Smashed growth near the scene indicated a possible struggle. They found Lindy's purse. Her wallet was still inside, so we assume it wasn't a robbery."

"Do you think it was Alexander or Marcus?" She dropped his hands.

"We're not sure. A camera on the closest parking lot caught a blurry image of four people entering a work van. Two of them looked like an older couple under duress. The others wore sunglasses and hooded sweatshirts. Their body descriptions didn't indicate a likeness to either of our prime suspects, but those two have a history of hiring local help."

"Have either of them tried to contact you yet?" Freddie's head spun. She'd forgotten to breathe. Gulping air steadied her. The need to remain strong for whatever lay ahead rushed to her pounding heart along with fresh oxygen.

Kent's fist closed and opened. "I haven't heard anything, but we've managed to destroy or lose several cell phones since our journey began. If they sent messages to one of those devices, we wouldn't know. I can only hope they contact my office if they don't get an answer from the phone they used to threaten my family." He reached a hand toward her shoulder.

Freddie shrugged out of his reach and crossed her arms. "You will keep me up to date. I want to know everything you find. I will do what it takes to free my parents."

"I promise to share any information, but you will not make the decisions regarding freeing your folks or mine. Is that understood?" A frown crossed his face.

"We will see what happens." She clamped her jaw tight. Her effect on other lives was getting out of hand. His family was under threat. Her parents were in the hands of unknown kidnappers. The life she'd established as a teacher no longer existed, at least for now. She'd made her peace with God and knew heaven waited. If she sacrificed her life for others, that might solve everything. Amber had discovered Max's evidence against everyone. The names of the cybercriminals were exposed and they would stand trial. She could bargain with Alexander and Marcus for her parents' freedom and the safety of Kent's family. She'd give those creeps some possible codes until they found out she knew nothing. Then...

"By your expression, I see you're plotting your own plan, Freddie. That didn't work in the past and it won't work now. Alexander and Marcus are much more dangerous than they were before. They're getting desperate to get out of the country with Max's money before we catch them. Let my agency do what we need to do without you jumping ahead of us." He paused. His words came out softer. "I want you around. We lost our connection once. I'd like you to be part of my future. Let me help you be there." He pulled her closer, looking at her lips.

Freddie's knees wavered. She wrapped her arms around his waist. If he kissed her, she would relish it, but she wasn't going to change her mind about saving those in danger. She ducked her head to his chest as his face drew closer. Deception wasn't going to be part of her life again. She'd only promised to see what would happen and that was all she could give right now.

Beep, beep.

Freddie stumbled away from Kent's arms, leaving her missing his warm embrace. Victor honked again, reminding them that they needed to get moving before something else happened. Should she have given in to the kiss Kent's expression had hinted at?

No. Reacting to his offer would continue to put everyone in jeopardy. She focused on not thinking about his dream of a future. Danger was following them, and it was all her fault. She hurried to the SUV's backdoor. Kent chose to sit in the passenger seat next to Victor.

At least there would be no more temptation to lean into his strength. She turned her thoughts to possible scenarios that might bring an end to everyone's troubles. It didn't help that every other idea ended with Kent holding her tight, smothering her with kisses in a happy place. She should have kissed him and gotten that temptation out of her mind. Somehow, she didn't think that would have solved a thing, other than breaking her heart again.

Chapter Twenty

Tamera waved to Kent as she approached the vehicle. She handed him a set of keys. "You'll need these to open two different gates on the way to the retreat building. Make sure you lock them after you go through. Follow my wagon trail near that line of pines. It should be passable and you won't have to follow Carlton on the road." She grinned at both of them and winked as she stepped away and held open a gate.

Victor put the SUV in gear, and drove through the opening, covering Kent's groan. Tamera would be gossiping with Dianne about what had almost happened between him and Freddie. He couldn't believe they'd almost kissed. She'd had the good sense to duck her head at the last second. Kicking himself for being unprofessional, Kent focused on the faint path that led from the ranch house to the retreat center. Any romance needed to wait for the right time. The SUV bounced along the trail meant for an all-terrain vehicle or a horse-drawn wagon. He hoped the other vehicle transporting his family was faring better on the overgrown road that Carlton headed for with his bush hog.

Victor wore a grin as the vehicle jolted across an almost dry creek bed. "I'm having fun driving off road, Boss. We should include more of this in our driver's training."

Relief poured through Kent at the change in subject. "I'm sure you'd be glad to volunteer for teaching duty. Make sure you allow plenty of time to stop when we reach one of Tamera's gates." He grabbed the grip above his head and held tight.

They rounded a curve and skidded to a stop. The first gate stood a few inches from the front bumper.

Freddie gasped from the back seat.

Kent chuckled. "See what I mean?"

Victor said, "Sorry about that."

Kent climbed out and headed for the gate. As the sound of clumping hooves grew closer, he paused at the gate. A small mare with her belly bulging stepped closer and sniffed at him.

"Well, aren't you a friendly one." Kent rubbed the equine's soft ears and received a snort in return. "I doubt Miss Tamera would want me to let you through the gate with us." His heart cracked a little as thoughts of riding horses with Freddie long ago flashed across his mind.

Those were sweet times. The scent of fresh soap filled the air as

Freddie stepped closer. He breathed in the fragrance he'd ignored during their almost kiss. She'd done more than wash her hands at the ranch house. Everything about her smelled fresh and new... He looked forward to when they could start anew.

"Let me hold her halter while you two get the SUV through the gate. Hey, pretty momma." Freddie crooned to the mare while Kent slowly stepped away.

He waved for Victor to drive through and then closed the gate most of the way. Freddie gave the horse one last pat on its rump, heading the lumbering mare toward a grazing pasture near the edge of the trees. Another horse nickered, calling the equine forward. Freddie hurried Kent's way. His heart thudded in his chest as he let her squeeze between him and the gate. He padlocked the gate with a snap, temporarily locking up his feelings about one day loving Freddie again.

When he climbed back in the car the air seemed lighter. Freddie started chatting about the friendly animal and its future offspring. Victor slowed down and they managed to make it through two more gates, without crashing into them or bouncing out of their seats. The road widened as they pulled into the small yard of the retreat center. A welcome sign hung above the middle door of the log-framed building. A row of windows, interspersed with doors, indicated several rooms or gathering spaces within.

An open-fronted horse shed stood next to the structure with a couple of hay bales waiting for any animals that might come on a trail ride. One of the bales had broken open, indicating an animal had already enjoyed some of the hay. A fresh manure pile left Kent wondering if one of Tamera's horses had escaped her gates and made it to the shed. He hoped not. Having to deal with a loose horse in the midst of a battle wasn't something they needed. He lifted the key ring and looked for the one marked for the house.

"Freddie, wait in the car while we check the place out." Kent looked back and saw her nod. At least she wasn't arguing. He didn't know if that was a good sign or not, but he needed to do his job.

Pausing before entering the door, he listened. Nothing came from within. A few birds trilled nearby. He recognized the call of a blue jay, not his favorite bird, but one with amazing coloring. Victor stepped to his side as Kent twisted the key and swung the door open. They did a quick sweep with Victor heading left while Kent went down the hall to the right, and meeting back at the front door.

"All clear. The place looks great, Boss."

"I agree. Let's get our witness safely inside and wait on the others." Kent looked toward their empty car.

~~~~~
~~~~~

Freddie edged closer to the woods behind the horse shed. The flash of a white coat with dark spots on what might be a horse had disappeared from her side vision while she sat in the car. There was something wrong with the animal. She wasn't sure what, but instinct told her the animal desperately needed some help. It must be hungry since she thought it might have approached the partially eaten bale of hay before spotting her and hiding.

"Come here, sweet creature." She crooned in the same soft voice she'd used with the mare. Movement in the trees guided her closer.

"Freddie, where are you?" Kent's booming voice reached her at the same time the spotted equine heard him. The scrawny animal's eyes widened. It flicked long ears, before struggling deeper into the woods.

Freddie clenched her hands and turned back toward the front of the buildings. "I'm over here. There's a horse or maybe a mule in the woods. I was trying to coax him out when you bellowed."

"I wasn't bellowing. I told you to stay in the car. When I didn't see you, I had no idea whether someone took you or worse." His gaze seemed to bore into her eyes as he stepped into view and gripped both shoulders. Concern and maybe more was there as his hands released their tight hold and slid down her arms until he held her hands. "Please don't do that again."

Freddie lifted her chin and jutted it toward the woods. "I will try, but I think that animal needs our help. He was so thin that at first I couldn't tell if he was a forest creature or part of the horse family. After seeing his ears, he might be a mule, but I'm still not sure." She gave his hands a squeeze and dropped one as she pointed to where she'd last seen the animal.

Victor rounded the back of the building, his gun pointed toward the ground. He holstered it and grinned at their held hands. "I see you found her. I'll keep watch out front."

"No." Freddie heard Kent's voice echo hers.

"We've got a horse or mule running around. We need to locate it before we set up our snare. We don't want it to be a distraction." Kent nodded to Victor. "Check the horse shed and see if there is any rope or an old halter."

Victor returned with a lead rope that had seen better days. It would have to do.

Freddie provided the unique coloring of the equine. "He entered the woods over here. I doubt he got very far." She led them to where the animal had disappeared. The trail of broken brush and a few pieces of hay were easy to follow. Freddie was thankful when Kent didn't object as she took the lead.

Within five minutes she saw the spotted mule tangled up in a vine that wrapped around one of his hooves. He snorted and nipped at them as they tried to free him. Freddie spoke comforting sounds to him as Kent pulled off his outer shirt and tied it around the mule's eyes. Victor pulled a knife from his pocket and cut the vine free. They clipped the worn lead rope onto a halter the animal still wore and led him back to the horse shed. Despite his weakened condition, the mule displayed a stubborn attitude, balking at their efforts until they brought him to hay and water in the shed.

Freddie's heart broke as she studied the miserable mule. His ribs stuck out. In addition to his unique spots, several scars marred his coat, indicating cuts from some kind of abuse. Blood on his rump showed evidence of recent harm. A lump protruded from under his skin in one area. Someone had treated the animal wrong and that didn't sit right with her.

"Is there anything we can do for him?" she asked.

"Tamera mentioned that the neighboring farm is a rescue ranch for mules. Maybe he came from there."

"I hope this isn't the way they treat their mules." Anger rose in Freddie's chest.

Kent laid an arm across her shoulders. "Let's hope he's a recent acquisition."

His comfort wrapped around her like a warm blanket. Her shoulders relaxed. "Maybe Tamera can check him out before we send the mule back, if that's the case."

"We need to do something fast. I hear the rumble of Carlton's bush hog in the distance. It won't be long until my family and an army of agents arrive in these woods."

"Do you want me to stay here with old Sylvester the mule while you walk to the road to meet the others?" Victor reminded them of his presence.

"Why did you call him that?" Kent asked.

"He reminded me of a kid's book I once read." Victor scuffed his toe on the ground.

"I know that one. It's illustrated by one of my favorite children's artists. I've modeled my style of drawing after his." Freddie's mind wandered to her books. She'd never thought of using a mule in her books. She did enjoy reading the Marty Mule's Musings comic strip in the newspaper she purchased periodically back in Lee County. She should leave the mules to that illustrator and not infringe on their specialty.

Kent waved a hand in front of her face. "Hey, Freddie? Are you coming with me or staying here with the mule and Victor?"

She gulped. Staying in place would be the safer choice on more than one count, but at the same time she didn't want to lose sight of Kent. His white undershirt clung to his toned body. His regular button-down shirt still hung over one arm, after he'd removed it from Sylvester the mule's eyes. "I'll follow you." Her voice sounded breathy in her own ears.

When she didn't add anything right away, Kent's eyebrows rose. She cleared her suddenly tight throat and continued. "I want to see if your grandchildren have arrived safely."

Kent nodded and held out an elbow. Freddie grabbed on as they headed toward the distant sound of brush breaking into pieces. A flicker of doubt entered her mind. Would their safe house be far enough away from where the trap would be set up?

Chapter Twenty-One

Kent led Freddie through the forested area surrounding the retreat center and located a path heading toward the grinding sound of the bush hog. Weeds had partially overtaken the trail, making him thankful for the cowboy boots he always wore. Riding had been one of the favorite things he and Freddie did when they dated. He'd never realized the footwear might have symbolized the hopes and dreams they'd shared. Wearing them had become a habit. He wanted to deny the root inspiration for that habit.

Moving on with someone new who hadn't disappeared from his life had provided the family he craved. Loving his wife with all his heart, he'd pushed thoughts of Freddie into the past. Their son and grandchildren had filled their lives with purpose until cancer had taken Madeline away.

Freddie released his arm when they cleared the tree line. An open field of wild growth pushed into their trail, making walking side-by-side difficult. He led, thankful again for his solid boots providing protection from snakes or a twisted ankle. For once, Freddie didn't argue or try to go ahead. Noise from the bush hog grew louder. The sound had seemed loud when they left the retreat center. Now it blasted in his ears from what looked to be at least a half-mile away. He hoped Carlton wore ear protection.

He held up a hand to halt Freddie and turned to face her. "Let's wait here until Carlton finishes. We don't need to damage our hearing."

"I agree. I'm just glad Carlton's road was farther from the retreat building than I thought. The noise was deceptive." She stepped closer when a grasshopper flew across their path.

Kent laughed. "You aren't afraid of a little bug, are you?"

"Not grasshoppers. Stinging insects are another matter." Her face paled.

"Is there something I need to know?" Trepidation crossed Kent's thoughts. She'd neglected to tell him another detail of her life.

"I should be fine, but..." She chewed her bottom lip as Kent waited.

"But what?"

She shuddered and hugged her waist. "In the past few years, I've had some reactions to stinging insects. Nothing dangerous has happened yet, but my doctor suggested I have an antihistamine around in case of an emergency."

"So, please tell me you have something with you." He held his voice down to a low roar. An allergic reaction would complicate things if it happened.

She put her hands on her hips and glared. "It wasn't like I had time to bring anything with me since you arrived at my house a few days ago and we rushed off. Besides, so far my reaction has been limited to a rash."

Kent lifted a silent prayer for her protection and closed his eyes in thought. "Maybe Chelsea has the right pills in the first-aid kit she usually travels with. She keeps it around for possible family illnesses and accidents. I've seen her use it more than once."

"Your daughter-in-law is a good woman. I'll check with her when we see your family."

"I hope they've already arrived." Kent checked his watch. The other car should have made it to where Carlton was clearing debris. "It wouldn't surprise me if they went ahead of him since there was once a road there. Carlton was widening the path so our RVs could get through easier."

As he spoke the sound of mowing faded. Children's laughter mingled with adult voices. Kent hurried through the last hundred yards with Freddie trailing behind him. His grandsons ran toward him when he reached the clearing.

"Hi, Grandpa. We got to ride on a roller-coaster road. It bumped up and down." Mason hugged Kent while Jordan zigzagged past him to Freddie's open arms.

"Hey, Miss Freddie. Can you write a story about a tractor with a big mower on it like that one over there? I really like tractors."

She hugged the boy and nodded as a smile crossed her face.

Kent wanted to cheer on the child's affection, but knew they needed to proceed with caution. He prayed they'd all walk away from this situation in one piece. However, guaranteeing anything was impossible until this case came to an end. Kent didn't know what the legal system would demand of Freddie and how many criminals they would apprehend. Until then, he needed to keep his mind on the business at hand.

"Boys, stay here with Miss Freddie for a minute. I need to talk to your mom and my agents."

Mason rolled his eyes. "Grown-up talk is boring. We'll make up stories with Winnie, I mean Miss Freddie until you get back."

Kent ruffled the boys' hair and then hustled over to speak with Chelsea first. "Glad to see you made it. Please tell me you brought your first-aid kit and have some antihistamines inside."

Chelsea pulled one of her bags from the SUV trunk. "I believe I have some. Let me check though." She unzipped the luggage and pulled out the familiar padded lunch box that Kent recognized as her medical bag. She lifted a blister pack of pink pills from the container. "Is this what you need?"

"Take those to Freddie and see if the pills will work if she has an insect bite reaction."

Chelsea's eyebrows lifted. "I hope she doesn't have a serious problem. We don't have anything stronger like an anaphylactic pen."

"She indicated only having milder reactions as of now." Kent hoped she'd told the truth. He watched Chelsea walk toward Freddie and the boys, before heading over to consult with his agents.

"How was your ride here?" Kent faced the two Virginia agents, and their driver, local agent Bart Matthews.

"We took the long way around and didn't have any interference. The hardest part was maneuvering this trail that's supposed to be a road. Whenever we hit a dip, your grandsons seemed to enjoy bumping up and down in the third seat of the SUV. I wasn't sure if the shocks would survive the rough road." Bart's shaking head conveyed dislike of either the driving conditions or the grandsons' antics.

"I was glad to see your agent come along with his bush hog after we arrived. The freshly cleaned road and the area he cleared out for our camping sting will work well to draw in the criminals." Jared turned to face the open space. "There should be plenty of room here for a couple of RVs."

"Carlton's been off on medical leave. Helping us by mowing has given him something to contribute. I may have him help out at the safe house at the retreat center if we don't get enough agents to run this event." Kent knew the injured agent wanted to help. Having him man the familiar building would be a good placement if the need called for his help. As they spoke, Carlton started up the tractor and rattled down the road, mowing the opposite side as he headed back to his sister's home.

"Do you think the retreat center will work for keeping the civilians safe?" Angela asked Kent.

"It looks great. We need to move my family and our witness there as soon as possible. I'd like to get them out of here before everyone arrives. We have one problem though. A malnourished mule showed up at the building. We don't need it getting loose and interfering with our op. Victor stayed behind to keep the building secure and mind the mule. I'll give Carlton's sister a call and ask her to contact the owner of the mule ranch next door and see if the animal belongs to them. I hope she has their number." A shout from Jordan distracted Kent. His grandson was jumping around and pointing to something behind his grandpa's back.

Angela laughed as they turned in the direction the child pointed. "I don't think that will be necessary. It looks like one unhappy neighbor just arrived on horseback, or should I say mule back."

~~~~~

Freddie grabbed Jordan and Mason's hands to keep them from running toward the long-eared equine. The animal looked in great health and the rider kept the blonde mule in perfect control as they drew nearer. Freddie couldn't tell if the woman was terrified or angry. Either way, the mule owner looked displeased as she rode closer to the cluster of agents standing between the woman and Freddie's two young fans.

"What's going on here? This road hasn't been used in a long time and the noise is making my animals restless." The woman's voice shook. Freddie recognized the rider's false bravado. The sudden pawing of the mule and flicking of its ears gave further indication that the rider's words were braver than her thoughts.

Kent held out his badge. "We're conducting a federal operation here this week on your neighbor's property. We have their permission to be here. We promise not to interfere with your ranch. As long as you keep your animals close to home in the next few days, there shouldn't be any problems. We'll be camped less than a week and then we'll be gone."

"Good." She gave a curt nod and pulled her reins to the side, indicating a return to her property.

Freddie called out to stop her. "Are you missing a mule? We found a sickly-looking fellow at one of the buildings on this property."

"Does he have spots on a white coat?" The woman's expression showed interest and concern.

"I think his coat is white with dark spots. He's pretty dirty looking." Freddie wished they'd had time to clean up the poor animal, but the mule didn't seem to want their help when they captured it.

"Take me to him. He's new to us and ran away two days ago."

"We're going there soon. We could take you." Freddie bent her head to indicate Chelsea and the boys.

Kent nodded. "This is Freddie. She knows the path to take." He turned to Angela and Jared. "You two go with them. I'll let you know your next order after this lady takes her mule home."

"The name is Leah."

"Hi, Leah. Do you mind if the boys pet your mule?" Freddie watched the woman's shoulders relax.

"Sure. This is Blondie. She's a gentle creature who loves attention." Leah made a quick chirping sound and gave a slight tug on the reins. The mule lowered her face close enough for the boys to give it a quick rub.

"Nice mule. Her ears are so soft." Awe spread across Mason's face.

"Can I ride her?" Jordan wrapped his arms around Blondie's nose until she gave a snort.

Leah chuckled. "Maybe, after you take me to my runaway."

The boys gathered their backpacks. Chelsea followed them with a
~~~~~

small bag of her own after Kent promised to have the rest of their belongings delivered later. Freddie led them toward the path she'd recently traversed. The blister pack of antihistamines in her pocket added to her confidence as she pointed to the trailhead. Angela insisted on going first with Jared following in the rear. He made a joke about having to pick up after the mule and they all laughed.

Halfway through their trek the boys complained about being tired. After several bouts of whining, Leah allowed them to take turns riding with her on Blondie. Freddie's feet reminded her she'd walked the trail to the retreat center twice and wished she could take a turn on Blondie too. She missed having Kent by her side and needed a distraction.

When the trail widened, Freddie dropped back near Leah, her current saddle mate, Jordan, and Blondie. "What made you want to rescue mules?"

"Long-ears are hardworking animals. Abuse may occur because of their willingness to go beyond their limits. I decided to make a difference. Some people call them stubborn, but I enjoy their intelligence."

"Maybe Miss Freddie could write a story about your mules." Jordan fiddled with Blondie's mane.

Leah's shoulders tightened. Blondie let out a sound halfway between a bray and a whinny.

"Jordan, remember we agreed to keep that quiet for now."

"Sorry, Miss Freddie." The boy's head bent toward his chest.

"Well, now that you've shared everything, I thought about it, Jordan, but there's already a nice comic strip about a mule. I can't take someone else's ideas. Sticking with my own characters is much better." Freddie couldn't help but wonder why Leah released a long breath.

Leah looked over at Freddie. "So, you're a writer?"

"Yes, I've done some children's books. I like my privacy though, so I use a pen name." Freddie was relieved when Leah only nodded and urged her ride forward.

They walked in silence, then Blondie lifted her head and let out a whimpering sound that faded into a whistle. An answering call came from down the trail. Relief filtered through Freddie's tired muscles. The other mule and retreat center must be close.

"Identify yourselves. I'm a federal agent."

"It's Freddie, Victor. I've brought Kent's family and others with me, including someone to rescue Sylvester. How's our mule doing?"

Victor stepped into view. "He's been making noise since you left but hasn't minded nibbling on the hay we found." He stepped over to Leah. "I hope you haven't been abusing Sylvester."

She glared at the agent. "Never. He's new to my ranch and ran away. Give us a year and he will be healthy again."

The strength in Leah's voice surprised Freddie. Apparently, the woman wasn't timid when it came to speaking out on behalf of her rescues. Angela and Jared stepped forward and introduced themselves to the local agent as they all headed for the horse shed. Leah dismounted and suggested Chelsea and the boys watch from the safety of the other building.

Freddie observed as Leah approach Sylvester with a crooning voice and a handful of treats taken from Blondie's saddlebag. Fifteen minutes later, Leah had the runaway mule tethered to her saddle horn and began leading him back down the trail to Kent's headquarters. Jared followed her at a distance, saying he was heading back to help at the RVs. Victor and Angela remained at the retreat center. Freddie's thoughts wandered to Kent, wondering if he had any more leads on her parents' whereabouts after they disappeared on a different trail.

Chapter Twenty-Two

Kent stepped into one of the two RVs. Headquarters had provided the vehicles, but not the manpower. Only three more agents arrived with the campers. He might not have a choice when it came to asking for Carlton's help protecting his family and Freddie. There wasn't a question about whether the ailing agent would agree, but Kent had concerns about whether the man was ready.

He sank into the bench facing the RV's table. The tech crew had turned the dining space into a computer station. The satellite dish on the roof provided a local connection with plenty of data to reach others using the phone or computer. A bank of high-powered two-way radios sat on chargers. He'd make sure his team had the devices by tomorrow morning for widespread communication when they dispersed across the ranchlands. He picked up a pen and started making a list on the notepad sitting in front of the computers. The first thing on the list: contact his office and thank Dianne for providing the pad of paper. He needed to know if his secretary had new information on the case and the status of Freddie's parents.

Connecting the wifi calling on his phone to the satellite dish, he dialed Dianne and waited for her to answer. The phone went to voicemail.

"Hey, Dianne. Give me a call as soon as you get this message. It's Kent." He drummed his fingers after disconnecting. Dianne didn't miss calls. She must be in the ladies' room or on another line with someone important.

His phone buzzed, indicating two missed texts. One was from Landon. He opened that message first. The agent had been with Agent Graham Crusher and Amber Whitney when they'd taken down Martin the mole and uncovered the list of cybercriminal names.

Stopping by home for a sec. Heading to RVs by nightfall. Dianne caught me up.

Super. They had another person on the team to help capture Alexander and Marcus. Kent hoped for more, but God had provided a good, solid team. He remembered the time God asked Gideon to limit the number of his army and then the biblical judge went on to defeat the Midianites. Praying for a similar success and making a good plan gave

Kent all the encouragement he needed.

The other text was from his son. Kent let Lachlan know the following afternoon would be a good time to spread information on social media, leaking the story that he and Freddie had retreated to camp in RVs on the back road.

Kent pulled his notepad closer and doodled out scenarios for his small army to deal with the men who sought to capture Freddie. He wanted to make it difficult for those two criminals by dissuading other crooks from joining them. He dialed Dianne again and this time the call went through.

"Hey, Boss. I'm sorry. I was on the other line with the police out in Arizona. They received a ransom call, if you can call it that."

"Let me guess, they want us to give up Freddie in exchange for her parents." Kent dreaded Dianne's answer.

"That's the gist of their demands. The message indicated that the exchange could take place in Ohio."

"Good. They're getting close to our snare and I prefer they come without any extra help. Let's put them in a bind. I want the names and faces of Max's cybercriminal ring broadcast on the news and social media, especially Alexander and Marcus. Tell the world that anyone associating with those two at-large criminals will face similar charges."

"I'll get on that right after we hang up, Boss. How are things on your front?"

"We're a little low on manpower, but it looks like you saw Landon and gave him our location. We have the three agents you sent with the RVs, two Virginia agents, Victor, and Bart, along with Carlton. With God's help, I pray we can accomplish what we want to do."

"Do you really think Carlton is ready to return to service?" Dianne questioned.

Kent hesitated before answering. "I'm not sure. Maybe this will boost his confidence. He can at least guard Freddie and my family back at the retreat center. I'll put another agent with him and then place the other operatives near or in the RVs. We'll work out the details after Landon gets here. If I had another man, I wouldn't worry about it."

"I didn't hear you mention Nora Levigne. She was the agent assigned to bring Melissa up to you. Have they arrived?"

A shiver coursed through Kent's body. He'd concentrated on the upcoming plan and missed double-checking on his foster grandchild's whereabouts. "Do you know if they were headed to the ranch house, the retreat center, or the RVs?"

"I gave Nora directions to all three places in case there was a problem. If she isn't with you, then I'm hoping she made it to the ranch house and is headed to the retreat center from there with Melissa."

"Get on the phone with Tamera or Agent Levigne. Now. I want to know their location." Kent disconnected the phone and slapped it down on the table. One more complication. Make that two. He'd post an agent at the ranch house to protect Tamera. He'd suggest the rancher move to the retreat center, but knew she would insist on staying at the ranch to care for her horses. Kent's fingers rapped out a disjointed rhythm as he waited for his phone to ring. When the call came through, he answered immediately.

"Please tell me they are okay." Kent couldn't keep harshness from ringing loud and clear into the cell.

"All is well. They stopped at the ranch house and Tamera put Melissa on a horse for a short ride. Nora said they'd wrap things up and come straight to whichever site you tell them to head for."

"Tell Nora to call me. I need to talk to her directly." Kent ground his teeth.

"Calm down, Boss. She was making the child happy. There's no need to take her head off." His secretary's voice had a soothing effect.

"I wasn't planning on taking anyone's head off."

Dianne's pause suggested otherwise. "Are you sure? Your voice had an edge to it that I've not heard before."

Kent released a huff of pent-up air. "You're right. I'll calm down, but I need to talk to her about where to head next, so have her call." He signed off with Dianne and gave Landon a quick text regarding his situation. Kent's mind was working overtime. If Landon hadn't left town yet, he could pick up Melissa, leaving Agent Levigne free to stay with Tamera for protection duty.

Ping.

I'm halfway there. Stopped to grab a burger. What's up?

Stop by the ranch house, pick up Melissa, and bring her to the RV camp.

Kent tapped out his reply and waited only seconds before Landon replied.

Will do.

The phone rang. This time the caller identified herself as Agent Levigne. Kent steadied his voice. "Nora, please update your status and that of Melissa."

"Yes, sir. We are at the ranch house with the owner, Tamera. Melissa begged to take a short horse ride. We will head out right now to wherever you need us to go as soon as you give the order."

"I have decided that I want you to stay with Tamera on protection duty during this operation. Landon will arrive soon to escort Melissa directly to me." Kent resisted the desire to remind the woman about following orders. It was best that she wouldn't be working directly with him for now. He'd had enough stress for one day.

~~~~~

Freddie sat with Kent's grandsons, drawing at the retreat center's table. The boys had shared paper and pencils with her. Her shoulders relaxed as tension flowed away and the thrill of creating released her mind from most of her worries. She silently lifted her parents' safety and gave it to the Lord. God's help was the only thing she could hope for at the moment. She had to trust Him. Otherwise...

Mason leaned over to look at Freddie's doodles."Is that Carlton's tractor with a face?"

"It sure is. I like using machines for my characters." In her mind they were more fun and easier to draw than people and most animals.

"How come they called that mower-thingy a bush hog?" Jordan lifted his pencil from his sketch and met Freddie's gaze.

"I wondered the same thing. Maybe they call it a hog because it gobbles up the weeds." She made a chomping shape with her fingers and wiggled them in the air.

"You should draw the bush hog with a pig face." Jordan's comment made laughter bubble up in Freddie's chest. The three of them giggled together as she penciled a snout on the machinery's likeness.

A conversation erupted from outside. Freddie hushed the boys and waved them toward a door leading to an interior hallway where they waited to see what might happen. Angela's voice sounded close to the door when they heard a knock.

"Hey, everyone, we have a friend outside. Melissa has arrived." Angela swung the door open and a young girl ran in and embraced both the boys. Beads clicked together from multiple braids adorning her head. The trio bounced around the table for a few moments before their activity evolved into a game of tag.

Chelsea entered the room from the hallway. "Melissa. It is so good to see you."

"Mama Russell." The girl rushed to hug her former foster mother. "I miss you, but I'm so happy to be living with the Hallmark family. That's my last name, since they adopted me. We live in a big house now and have two dogs. We have a baby and a new brother too."

Freddie watched the happy reunion. She'd never had a child of her own, though many students admired her and had claimed a piece of her heart, starting with Amber. It was obvious having family was a different
~~~~~

kind of relationship that she had never experienced, unless Kent invited her to share with him one day.

"Don't look so sad, Miss Freddie. After we tell Melissa about you, she's going to love you just like we do." Mason pulled on her hand and led her toward his foster sister.

Jordan grabbed her other hand. "Hey, Melissa. You have to meet our new friend, Miss Freddie. She's got a secret that we can't share, but Grandpa likes her a lot. Maybe she will be our new grandma."

Heat rushed from Freddie's chest and up her neck. She would have covered her warm cheeks if the two boys weren't dragging her forward by her hands. Chelsea looked shocked.

Melissa shrugged as if a new relationship was not a big deal and turned toward the two youngsters. "If you boys tell me the secret, I'll share some of Miss Dianne's treats." She held up a shoulder bag and rattled the goodies inside.

"I don't mind sharing. I'm..." Freddie started to reveal her secret, but the two boys interrupted.

"She's Winnie Gee!" Jordan exclaimed.

Mason pushed his brother aside and pointed up at her. "She writes books."

Jordan poked his head under his brother's arm. "Miss Freddie draws the pictures too. She's been teaching us how to draw."

"Why do you call her Freddie if she is Winnie Gee?" Melissa asked.

Chelsea laid a hand on Melissa's shoulder. "Her real name is Winifred Grimsley. Friends call her Freddie, but she uses Winnie Gee for her books because she wants to keep it a secret."

"Oh." Melissa leaned her head to the side and tapped her chin. "If I wrote books, I think I'd want to tell everyone. We had an author come to school this year and I got her autograph. My adopted grandmother draws pictures too. I don't have her autograph, but I think I'll ask for it next time I see her. Sometimes Grandma goes to shows and shares her art. You could meet lots of kids and teach everyone how to draw. That would be fun."

"You are a wise young lady, Melissa. After our adventure here, I hope that I can share my secret." Freddie knew the child had a point. She was ready to share her career with others. Hiding hadn't been the best choice. Letting her light shine after the federal agents caught Alexander and Marcus would be a priority.

The sound of a radio squawking interrupted her thoughts. Everyone turned toward Angela, who'd been observing their interactions.

"What was that?" Freddie's gaze met the agent's.

"We have two-way radios for communicating with the boss. Landon brought them when he delivered Melissa to the RVs." Angela tapped her waistband where the device rested. "The operation starts tomorrow afternoon, but everyone here will be fine. You children don't have to worry about a thing." She grinned at the boys and then turned toward Freddie, who saw the worry creasing Angela's forehead.

Chapter Twenty-Three

"That's what I have planned if you think you can handle the job." Kent spoke into the radio and waited for Carlton's reply.

"I'll be there first thing in the morning. Guarding your family is the least I can do since I allowed Jade's kidnapping." Carlton's voice cracked.

"There's no need to keep worrying about her. She's safe at home by now and well guarded. I'm more worried about your self-confidence."

"I'm fine, Boss."

Kent shook his head, glad Carlton couldn't see his face. "I know you will be. Victor and a Virginia agent named Angela will be there to assist. Victor will stay with them until you get there, and then he will report back to me where all the action should start happening in the next day or so."

"I'll pack for several days and bring the gear I have here at home. I'll take the ranch's ATV up the trail to the retreat center. Thanks for having someone here to protect my sister and her ranch. I wouldn't have agreed unless someone was with her."

Tamera and Nora protested in the background, saying two strong women didn't need Carlton's help.

"Understood. Family comes first." Kent sent up a prayer for protection of all the families involved. "Thank you again for being willing to step up and help. Nothing will be official because you haven't gone through all the red tape required for coming back. I'm hoping the criminals will take my bait and you won't see any action. I asked for backup, but didn't get what I wanted."

"You may not have the numbers, but the names you mentioned are some of the best agents in our locale."

"That's true, Carlton. You are included in that count." Kent almost added *for now*. He couldn't promise a permanent return beyond the current situation.

Carlton paused. "I better go pack my gear." His voice lacked the confidence Kent had longed to hear from his recovering agent.

A knock on Kent's door brought his attention to the meeting that would take place soon. The RV rocked from side-to-side as the agents climbed up stairs and took seats in the small living area. Kent stayed seated at the computer-filled table but he slid to the edge of the seat so he could see the agents sitting shoulder-to-shoulder on the couches lining both sides of the camper. Landon sat in the passenger's seat and swiveled back to face the group. Anticipation filled the man's face. He'd been part of the team that took down Victoria and her henchman. Landon had confided earlier about wanting to see an end to the case because of that involvement.

Kent nodded to him. "Please share what you've learned so far about the MAX Enterprises criminals."

"Graham, Max's daughter Amber, and I captured the ringleader, Victoria, and several of her henchmen. We have a recording provided by the late Max Whitney revealing the names of everyone involved in the cybercriminal group, including Marcus and Alexander. The agency arrested most of the perps, except for the two men that we plan to capture in the next few days." He turned to Kent.

"We are keeping our prime witness, Winifred Grimsley, in protection back at the retreat center located on this property. Tomorrow at noon we'll start placing hints on social media that Miss Grimsley and I are hiding in these RVs. A family member will 'accidentally' make the location known. The crooks have indicated that they think Miss Grimsley has knowledge of a code that will access hidden funds, allowing them to escape to another country. I assume they are aware that we have their names and have arrested many of their compatriots."

"So, what's the plan, Boss?" Sarah, the one female in the group asked.

"I'd like to have you stay in one of the RVs impersonating our witness. Be ready to be on the offensive if they try to come inside, but know we'll have your back. Keep the shades drawn so they can only make out that you are female. I'll have you communicate with Miss Grimsley on speaker so they hear her voice. We'll record that conversation and others, so you can replay one every few hours."

"What about the rest of us?" Leon, who'd driven one of the RVs, asked.

"We will need a perimeter set up with an advance warning team near the road leading here. The rest will station themselves near the RVs, ready to apprehend the suspects."

"Are there any complications we need to be aware of?" Steve, the other Ohio agent, leaned forward.

"I'm hoping they will come without a team of reinforcements. The other variable is that we believe they are holding Miss Grimsley's father and stepmother for ransom," Kent said.

"That's a big complication. Is she aware of this, and what is her reaction?" Landon met his boss's gaze and crossed his arms.

Kent swallowed. "She doesn't know, as of right now. I'm afraid she might take things into her own hands and try to make a sacrificial move."

Jared raised his eyebrows. "Are you sure that's the best thing? From what I saw in Virginia, I think she could handle the news."

"I'll give the idea of sharing some thought. I've been tied up with one situation after another since I got the call about her parents. I really haven't had time to think about anything beyond setting up this operation." Kent dismissed the flash of guilt that crossed his thoughts. "Are there any other questions?"

Shoulders raised and lowered. Others shook their heads. Landon yawned.

"Then I suggest you claim a bed, couch, or floor in one of the RVs and get a good night's sleep. I'll keep watch for a few hours and then wake one of you to take over." Kent needed the time to think. Was he making a mistake by not telling Freddie about her parents? Her earlier reaction to just the possibility of kidnapping scared him more than he wanted to admit. He didn't want her running from him again, even if it was to save her family.

~~~~~

Freddie helped tuck Mason and Jordan into bed and left their mother and Melissa to hear their prayers. She had some praying of her own to do, but decided to enjoy some fresh night air before heading for her own room in the retreat center. Angela sat outside, chatting with someone on one of the radios.

"Here comes Freddie right now. I'll let you speak to her in private." The female agent mouthed Kent's name and vacated her chair.

Freddie reached for the device and fumbled with the buttons until Angela showed her how it functioned.

"Hey, Kent. How's RV life?" She watched Angela stretch and start walking around the clearing in front of the retreat center.

"All is quiet for now. The action should start tomorrow afternoon. I do have something to share about your parents and need you to promise not to do anything on your own."

Freddie's pulse sped up. "Were they kidnapped?"

"The police in Arizona received a ransom note. The culprits know we're in Ohio and want to make an exchange here for the codes they think you have."

"Codes I don't have." She fisted her hand and pounded on the chair arm. "I might as well give up and let them take me until I can figure out what they want."

"No. You need to let my agency capture them at the RVs, after we leak the location. Your job is to stay safe. I don't want to lose you again."

Holding one hand to her chest, Freddie fumbled with the speaking button before she reconnected. "I don't know what to say. I'm hoping for a future together too. I'm sorry I made the wrong choice years ago."

"The past is gone. The future involves keeping you safe until this case is over. After that we can make plans, if you're still interested."
~~~~~

She leaned back in the chair. "Of course I'm interested. I always was. Trouble got in the way, and I thought I was protecting you."

"Then allow me to protect you now. Instead of running, use the time to get to know my family," Kent said.

She hesitated before replying, "Okay." She prayed she could keep her promise, but there were so many variables.

"I'm thinking about heading your way first thing in the morning to make sure Angela and Carlton are all set to keep you safe. When do you think you'll wake up? I'd love to have a few moments with you." The two-way radio crackled as Kent's words made her heart do summersaults.

"I rise with the sun or earlier. Even in summer, I can't break the teacher hours of waking early and getting to work." Seeing him in the morning would make waking something to look forward to instead of a chore.

"Good. Maybe we can have a few minutes to take a walk before I head back to the RVs." The warmth in his voice filled Freddie with hope.

"I look forward to seeing you." Her voice came out breathier than she'd intended, but it felt nice to be wanted.

They signed off after Kent arranged for her to talk to Sarah early the next morning for some recorded conversations. Freddie waved to Angela, who had wandered away to give them privacy.

The agent grinned as she approached and retrieved the two-way radio. "Did Kent give you good news? You look happy." She plopped down in a white plastic chair, identical to Freddie's.

"Actually, there was upsetting information about my dad and stepmom. A ransom note came in to the authorities out west." Freddie hugged her arms around herself as she updated Angela on the situation.

"That's too bad, but you need to give us time to enact Kent's plan." Angela scanned the surrounding forest before giving Freddie a look that made the art teacher want to squirm. "I'm guessing there was more to your conversation, since you were smiling after your chat ended."

Freddie looked away before she faced the woman who had become her friend. "If we make it through this ordeal, there's a strong chance that Kent and I may have a future together."

Angela laughed. "From what I've seen, your future is secure. The man adores you and so do his grandsons. You might have to work on his daughter-in-law, but I'd say you're practically a member of the family already."

A chuckle came from behind them. "This daughter-in-law has no problem adding Miss Freddie to the family." Chelsea stepped out from behind the screen door and pulled another plastic chair closer to the other two women. "You were all the boys could think about before and during their prayers. Even Melissa is impressed. She's come a long way since we first fostered the shy little waif who was afraid of her shadow. Her confidence has grown even more after the Hallmarks adopted her. Ginny was her teacher for two years and is now her mother."

Freddie welcomed the change of subject. "Tell me more about Melissa's new mother. She must be a blessed woman, able to solve the world's problems."

"Ginny is a wonderful person, but like the rest of us, she's had challenges. She's a teacher, like you. I think that gave her skills to overcome some complicated situations and deal with multiple children's backgrounds. But none of us is perfect. We have to trust God to see us through each day, pray for forgiveness, and ask Him what's best for our family. Including those we hope to add." Chelsea laid a hand on Freddie's wrist and gave it a squeeze.

"Thank you."

Nighttime chirps and calls rang in her ears as Freddie chatted with the women until Victor came to relieve Angela for the evening watch. Freddie headed off to her own bed with a yawn. While darkness covered the sky, dreams of a future with Kent, and worries for her parents swirled in and out of her thoughts.

Chapter Twenty-Four

Kent rose with the first hint of dawn. He'd set an alarm on his phone for an early start to check on Freddie. When he pushed the curtains aside from the RV window, shades of pink and purple brushed the morning sky. After his conversation with Freddie, he had stayed up until midnight before waking Jared to take a shift guarding their RV camp. Despite his lack of sleep, excitement for the chance to check on Freddie put him in a good mood. It would be nice to see his family, but his motivation for the day centered on the woman who'd changed his life in the past and present. He dressed and stepped around the others camped out in the front portion of the RV, before making his way down the camper's stairs.

"Good morning, Boss. Are you ready for action?" It appeared Landon had taken Jared's place during the early morning hours. The agent's hair was damp with morning dew.

"I will be, after I check in with my family back at the retreat center. Can you hold things down here until I get back?" Kent was anxious to get on his way and come back before information about their location became public.

"I'll take care of everything. Do you need someone to go with you? I noticed Steve is up and wandering around." Landon pointed a thumb over his shoulder to where the other agent stood doing some morning stretching.

"Good idea, Landon. I'll check with him." Kent wanted to go on his own but realized it would be better security to travel with a partner.

Steve and he were soon on their way, pushing through the narrow path in single file until it widened enough for them to travel side-by-side. He noticed evidence of the mule's passage from the other day and hoped it wasn't enough to lead the criminals to the hideout. Bees and horseflies lingered near a manure pile sitting in the middle of their path, reminding Kent of Freddie's possible allergy to stinging insects. He lifted a prayer for her protection and plodded ahead until they reached the edge of the retreat center's clearing. Hearing the sound of a motorized vehicle, Kent and Steve stepped back into the woods, prepared for the unexpected.

Kent spotted Victor taking a ready position on the closest side of the retreat center. Kent whistled a signal known to their group. Victor raised a thumb, acknowledging they would back each other up. Seconds later, a four-wheeler cleared the trail leading from the ranch.

They all relaxed when Carlton took off his helmet and ran fingers through his mussed hair. After cutting power to the vehicle, he called out his identification. Kent and the other agents stepped out from their hiding places.

"Glad to see you made it." Victor gave Carlton a slap on the back. Steve did the same. Carlton pulled a cane and a backpack from the vehicle and headed toward the building. The two active agents followed their limping friend to a circle of chairs in front of the retreat center.

Kent wondered if he'd get any privacy with Freddie, as she and his family piled out of the building and headed toward him. A yawning Angela stood in the doorway, watching as Kent's grandsons ran his way. The female agent turned to the side and joined the others gathered around the chairs. Kent accepted hugs from the boys and Melissa, before turning his attention to the two other women.

"Hi. I thought I'd stop by and see how everyone was doing."

"And take a walk with our Miss Freddie." Chelsea grinned at him like a Cheshire cat. "There's a short path along the backside of the house if you want some privacy." His daughter-in-law wasn't very subtle. "She's been up talking to your agent Sarah since dawn. I wonder if you were part of that conversation."

Kent shook his head.

"We like her, Grandpa," Mason added while Jordan bounced at his brother's side.

Melissa smiled and made a heart shape with her hands.

A fresh pink blush covered Freddie's face as she opened her mouth to speak. "Angela was a very effective interrogator after the conversation we had last night."

Chelsea hugged Freddie. "I'm glad I overheard their conversation and joined them to hear more. I've already started thinking Freddie will make a great mother-in-law if you give her a chance."

It was Kent's turn to feel the warmth of a blush coating his cheeks. "Whoa. Give us time to work things out. There's too much at stake with this ongoing case." He felt like frowning at the interference of his family. Instead, he held out an elbow toward Freddie. "I need that private walk now." He pulled her around the side of the building unsure whether to laugh, scream, or throw his hands in the air. "I'm so sorry."

"Hey, that's my line. I apologize for sharing too much during our girls' chat last night." Freddie closed her eyes and lowered her head. Wispy hair covered half her face.

"Don't worry about it. You need friends you can talk to, and I want to be your closest friend, once this case is over." Kent lifted her chin with his palm and ran a thumb across Freddie's cheek. Too many years had passed since he touched her face with longing in his heart. Feelings from long ago rushed over him, stripping away the past. He leaned closer and brushed her soft hair to the side before lightly kissing her upturned lips. Her long sigh spoke to his soul, but he stepped away, saying, "Enough for now."

Holding hands, they took the promised walk without speaking. Birds welcomed the morning with happy tunes. A pair of chipmunks crossed their path as they chased each other. Freddie and Kent stopped to stare at a pair of birds caring for their young. Kent wanted to join the morning chatter and declare his feelings, but today the criminals stood between them. Once they captured the crooks, and a trial took place, there might be time for more, if they all survived. Instead, he wrapped his hand tighter around hers and gave her a quick peck on the cheek. Hope was all he could promise.

~~~~~

A crackle from Kent's radio sent a chill down Freddie's arms. She froze in place as a female voice spoke.

"Everyone. This is Agent Nora Levigne. I know Kent's son wasn't supposed to leak your position until later, but it looks like trouble is heading your way. There is an off-road style SUV headed toward the RVs. We spotted the vehicle from a distance, but it looked like there might have been at least two people inside."

Kent dropped Freddie's hand. His sharp commands to the agents rang in her ears as he waved her back toward the building. Carlton stood near the shed and laid a hand on his holster. Angela came from the edge of the woods as the couple reached the front entrance to the retreat center.

At the door Kent kissed her forehead. "Get inside and stay away from the windows. Remain with my family and obey the agents." He gave her a look that brooked no argument. "I'm headed back to the RVs."

When Freddie closed the door, Kent's daughter-in-law and grandchildren already sat inside. Worry lines creased Chelsea's forehead, but it appeared she had chosen to distract her boys by directing them to their drawings.

"I'm going to draw Miss Freddie and Grandpa holding hands." Jordan leaned over his paper and started drawing stick figures standing close to each other. The child's tongue wrapped around his upper lip.

Melissa started drawing hearts on the piece of paper they'd shared with her.

"Ugh, you two." Mason wrinkled his nose. "That's too mushy. I want to go back to drawing machines that can talk."

"That's an excellent idea. Maybe we can figure out a story together." Freddie was glad for the change in subject.

"Yay. Are we going to use a bush hog?" Jordan lost interest in his stick figures. His expression begged for Freddie to include the machine.
~~~~~

"I'm sure we can find a way to work one in." Ideas for using the new character started forming in Freddie's thoughts. Creativity always helped her relax. The boys and Melissa talked over each other as she took notes and formulated an outline that might work.

A knock silenced their chatter. Jordan started to run for the door. Freddie grabbed his hand to stop him.

"Who's there?" she called.

"It's Angela. I'm coming in for a bite of lunch. You can let me in."

Freddie's stomach rumbled as her shoulders sagged in relief. Time had passed quicker with the distraction of coming up with story ideas. She hadn't realized it was close to noon. She unlocked the door and the agent entered. Freddie followed her to the kitchen, where they took sandwich materials from the provisions they'd brought with them. The scent of canned tuna wafted through the room as they mixed the seafood with mayo and spread it on bread.

Freddie closed the door to the room. "Have you heard anything over your radio?"

"Not much. The criminals haven't arrived at the RVs yet. Steve, Victor, and Kent did make it back. Speculation is that Alexander and Marcus knew about the back road from when their partner in crime, Martin, kidnapped Max's daughter, Jade. Maybe they have a plan of their own for setting up the trade-off in the same area. They definitely know you're in the greater northwest Ohio area after seeing us get off the plane."

"That will put them right on top of your operation when Kent's son posts his information." Freddie used the can opener on a container of canned chicken, figuring some might want a choice between the two meats.

Angela checked her watch. "It's almost noon, which was when the information about the campers was supposed to be shared. Hopefully those two suspects will have enough data connection to intercept the message."

The two women placed canned drinks, chips, sandwiches, and fruit cups out on trays. They carried the aromatic food to the table in the other room where the boys and Melissa sat drawing. Angela filled a paper plate with a tuna sandwich and chips. She grabbed a bottled drink and went outside. Carlton limped in fifteen minutes later and ate with the children as they finished up. Freddie was glad she'd made the chicken sandwiches after seeing Carlton wrinkle his nose at the tuna.

"Hey, Mr. Carlton. How did you hurt your leg?" Jordan stuffed chips into his mouth. His words came out mumbled and laced with crumbs.

Chelsea stacked a used napkin on her empty plate and shook her head. "Please don't be disrespectful to Mr. Carlton, and don't talk with food in your mouth."

"Sorry, Mom and Mr. Carlton." The youngster looked down.

"I don't mind sharing a few minor details." Carlton rubbed his leg. "I was chasing a bad guy and got hurt. I'm getting better now. Riding horses at my sister's ranch made me feel better."

"I got to ride one of your sister's horses on the way here. It was fun." Melissa smiled as she sipped juice from the fruit cup.

Mason laid his sandwich down. "I liked riding a mule the other day. Is that like riding a horse?"

"Their rides are probably close. I haven't ridden one, but I've heard mules can be stubborn. I think I'd rather be on a horse." Carlton pointed to the children's drawings. "Tell me about your pictures."

Freddie wanted to laugh. The man might make a good teacher if he gave up working for the federal agency. He knew how to answer without scaring the children and when to redirect their attention.

When his meal was over, Carlton stood. "I'm going to take a walk around the buildings. You kids take care of the ladies."

After the children helped clean the table, Chelsea suggested they take an afternoon rest in their beds. After several groans, they complied.

Freddie needed a break from the smell of tuna and decided to grab a quick breath of fresh air. She spotted Angela sitting in the chairs outside and joined her.

"I see you don't follow orders very well, Freddie." Angela smiled in spite of her comment.

"I needed a break from being inside, and it looked like you could use some company." Freddie eased into the chair and breathed in the pine scent. Pink buds peeked from an azalea bush next to the retreat center, adding a delightful visual effect.

"Waiting for action can be tedious, especially when the cell phone connections aren't the best." Angela tapped restless fingers on her useless phone and then pocketed the instrument. "I don't care for two-way radios. They're too noisy if you're trying to hide."

"Is there any news?" Freddie asked.

"We're on radio silence right now. Steve is taking a hike down the road to see if he can spot the men. We don't want them hearing our conversation if he gets close." Angela ran a finger around the circular speaker on the radio. "So, how was your walk this morning with the boss?"

Freddie spotted a deer near the edge of the woods. She needed a diversion of her own. Pointing toward the creature, she leaned close to Angela. "Look at the doe. Do you see any young ones with her?"

Angela shook her head. "I don't see any others, but she's a beauty."

The deer lifted her head from the ground and sniffed the air before bounding away from the *thump scrape* of Colton's cane and foot. He came around the corner and frowned.

"You need to be inside, Miss Grimsley. I can't lose another person on my watch."

"Sorry, I was just heading back in." Freddie hoped her expression came off as repentant. Relieved not to rehash her growing feelings related to the walk was a better description of her present reaction. As she reached for the door, the screech of two-way radios made her pause.

"Steve here. I'm almost back to the RVs. I found their vehicle about a mile from our camp. No one was there. Both camps get ready. It looks like they've taken to the woods." Heavy breathing indicated he was moving quickly.

"Get inside," Carlton snapped.

Freddie didn't argue.

Chapter Twenty-Five

Kent didn't like Steve's news. Not knowing where the two criminals were complicated his whole plan. His thoughts ran like a wildfire as he started rearranging where he needed his people to be.

Deciding to risk someone overhearing, he started barking commands. His first order went over the air via the radios. "Jared, take the SUV down and meet Steve on the road. See if you two can track those men from where Steve spotted their car. We need to know their location."

He stepped from the RV and waved to Bart, who had driven Kent's grandkids to the RV camp. "Get those keys to Jared, pronto, and then come back here to regroup with the others. Let everyone else know we're meeting in my temporary office in two minutes."

Kent picked up a piece of paper and started mapping out his thoughts. He had the three local agents who moved the RVs to their location: Sarah, Steve, and Leon. Victor and Bart had driven the SUVs in. Jared, Angela, and Carlton rounded out his Gideon's army. He didn't count Agent Levigne, though she'd done her part by sending the warning.

Steve and Jared were hopefully busy tracking by now. Angela and Carlton were at the retreat center. That left Victor, Bart, Sarah, and Leon. Sarah had recorded her chats with Freddie during the time it took him to walk back from the retreat center. The female agent was ready to play her role of talking inside the RV. Rushing feet bounded into the camper. The agents stayed standing, ready to move at Kent's orders.

"I want Sarah to stay in camp, following her original plan. Leon and Bart will be on guard duty here at this camp. I'll send Jared and Steve back here after they're through tracking."

Kent looked his trusted crew in their eyes. "I don't often work off of hunches, but I have a feeling that Victor and I should head to the retreat center." His guts and prayers all pointed to the need to be closer to his family and Freddie. The team of agents nodded in agreement. Sarah and her guards left to take their positions.

"Let me grab my supplies, and I'll be ready." Victor pulled his backpack from one of the overhead bins in the RV and ran a check on his handgun. "I have a rifle and other supplies in the SUV we left at the retreat center. They are available if we need them."

"I hope we don't, but let's get moving." Kent hefted his backpack to his shoulder and attached a holstered weapon to his belt. They left the RV and headed down the path. *Please Lord, I've lost her once. Keep her safe.* His heart thudded with exertion and worry as their feet pounded toward the other camp. Minutes felt like hours as they made their way in silence for at least a quarter of the trail. Sweat formed and ran down their faces. Kent swiped it aside and kept moving until Victor tapped him on the shoulder and pulled them to the side of the trail.

He pointed to waving grass in the distance and then laid a finger across his lips. They stood in silence. Something moved, but they couldn't make out what it was until a wild bray broke through the whispering grass.

"That crazy mule has gotten loose again." Kent almost laughed, but knew the animal would complicate things if it stood in a crossfire or interfered with their actions in another way.

Victor looked at Kent. "What do you want to do, Boss?"

"Leave the beast alone for now. Pray it doesn't get in the way of our actions against the criminals. We don't need the owner coming on the ranch looking for it either."

"How are you going to prevent her from interfering?" Victor asked.

"It took her several days to find him last time. Maybe the woman will look other places first."

"I hope you're right." Victor began leading them down the trail, stopping occasionally to scan the area and point out the mule's progress. "I could be wrong, but it looks like Sylvester the mule is headed in the same direction as us." He chuckled. "I might have spoiled him the other day, and he wants more."

"Great. Maybe he'll let you tie him up again. We don't need that animal running around the retreat center grounds if we have a confrontation." Kent stepped around Victor when the trail widened. He took the lead as he pushed toward his family's location. The urge to hurry grew in his mind. Kent upped his pace. His breath came faster. He either needed to do more workouts at the gym or retire. Retirement was looking better every day.

Victor laid a hand on Kent's shoulder. "Let's slow down. You need to catch your breath. Besides, we need to hear other people in the woods."

Kent knew the other agent was right. He took slower steps and listened to what was going on around him. They were getting closer to the retreat center and needed to be aware of others who might be approaching the building. The buzzing of bees and squawks of several large birds circling above them were the only noises he heard as they drew closer to the building, other than the occasional mule call.

A rush of wings broke the everyday sounds as a flurry of birds lifted from an area not far from the building. Someone shouted. A gun fired. The mule broke into a series of distorted brays and snorts. More voices filled the air.

Kent rushed forward. His heart raced. Victor ran with him. As they neared the retreat center, they split off into the woods with Victor going right and Kent left. Silence filled the air until the mule started bellowing again.

~~~~~

Freddie heard the commotion outside. It sounded like the mule was back and someone was hurt. Gunshot didn't speak well for whatever was happening. Neither did a man's low moans. She tapped on the door where Angela was resting.

Angela opened the door on the first knock and hopped out as she put a shoe on. "I heard. Let me see what's going on. Stay inside until you hear otherwise." The agent slid a curtain to one side and looked out. Her shoulders relaxed. "It looks like the mule has Carlton pinned to the ground." Laughter bubbled from her lips. "Let me make sure he's okay. Keep the door locked until I know for sure what happened." She stepped outside and Freddie clicked the lock closed. Chelsea peeked around the corner.

Freddie whispered what was happening. "Keep the children with you in one of the rooms until we know what's going on for sure. It may just be the return of that runaway mule."

Chelsea nodded and shut the door to the hallway. Freddie heard the children's pattering feet as they headed toward the far end of the building and slammed a door.

Seconds later, Angela's knock caught Freddie's attention as the agent spoke through the entrance to the building. "I'm going to need your help. That stinker of a mule knocked Carlton's injured knee out of joint. I'm afraid he's in bad shape. I think if we work together, we can get him inside."

"What about the gunshot?" Freddie pulled the door open and stepped out.

"He thought the mule was an enemy hiding in the woods and had his weapon ready to fire. It accidentally went off when the mule came running and knocked him down. At least the bullet didn't hit anything." Angela looked relieved.

"I'm glad too. I would hate knowing a person or animal got needlessly hurt," Freddie said

"Agreed, now let's get him in. I'll take care of guard duty until we can call for some reinforcements." Angela still looked sleepy from her short nap, but she lifted her chin as a determined expression filled her face.

Freddie nodded and headed toward Carlton, with Angela at her side. The mule stood over the man, nosing him with its whiskery mouth. She carefully coaxed the animal away while Angela bent over the man's leg.
~~~~~

The angle didn't look normal.

"Maybe we shouldn't move him." Freddie squatted next to Angela as Carlton moaned one more time and shut his eyes. "What do you..."

Someone grabbed Freddie's arms from behind at the same time a loud *thunk* knocked Angela's head to the side.

The female agent crumpled to the ground, falling across Carlton's chest.

Freddie's captor dragged her toward the woods. Someone stuffed a sweet-smelling rag into her mouth. As a sack went over her head, she caught a glimpse of Alexander's smirk. Marcus confirmed his presence by whispering something about the codes in her ear as he released one of her pinned arms to Alexander. With a man on each side, they pulled her away from safety and the family she'd come to love.

Her head spun as she tripped over sticks and rocks. She spat out the rag, leaving it wrapped around her chin inside the bag. If they had planned to knock her out, they weren't going to succeed, not if she could help it. Or maybe she should play along and start dragging her feet to make things difficult for them. She started slowing and mumbling as she leaned heavier onto their arms.

"Wake up, woman. I can't carry your weight and mine." Alexander's griping voice came from her right side.

"I thought you said this stuff would only make her woozy. I can't carry this woman through the woods if she passes out." Marcus' grumbles filled her left ear.

"Maybe I gave her too much. Let me get the rag off her mouth." Alexander pulled them to a stop and started fumbling with the ties at her chin.

"But what if she starts screaming?" Marcus wrapped his fingers around her arm and squeezed until it hurt.

"Then we'll threaten her parents' safety to keep her quiet." The strings loosened around her neck. They'd find out soon that the rag no longer remained in her mouth.

Freddie tried to pull away from Marcus' grip. "Where are my dad and Lindy?"

Alexander ripped the sack off her head. The scented rag fell from beneath her chin. "Ha. Looks like you're not as out of it as you've been pretending. Are you ready to give us the codes in exchange for the release of your old man and his lady?"

She wasn't going to make it easy for them, whether she had the codes or not. "I'll go with you if you take me to my parents. Then we can talk about codes." She jerked her arm away from Marcus and stared at him, daring him to disagree with her offer. The glare she gave the crook had shriveled up some of her toughest students' willfulness. She wasn't the scared little pushover she'd been back when she worked as Max's secretary.

He held up his hands and backed away. "Let's get a move on. It won't be long before your hound dog of a boyfriend starts sniffing out our trail." Marcus turned and Freddie followed, making sure to brush against or stomp on anything that might make their trail look disturbed. She'd leave as many clues as she could for her federal bloodhound boyfriend. Alexander didn't seem to notice her efforts as he followed her. The man might have even left a few clues himself without realizing his mistakes.

Marcus held out one arm. They stopped and listened. Voices echoed in the distance. Freddie recognized Jared's voice.

Alexander pulled Freddie to the ground and clamped his hand across her mouth as she listened to Jared speaking from yards away.

"It looks like they may be headed for the retreat center. We need to catch up with them before they get there." Jared's voice held confidence. Freddie knew better as she ground her teeth together, resisting the urge to bite Alexander's hand.

"I wonder how they knew about that place," the other agent replied.

Freddie pushed Alexander's hand from her mouth. She was tired of the nasty smell coming from his palm. Frowning at her captor, she pressed her lips together. For the sake of her parents, she chose to keep silent as the two agents walked the nearby trail.

"Martin did date the owner of the ranch. Maybe she took him there and he told Alexander and Marcus." Jared's voice seemed farther away.

A frowning Alexander held a warning hand out toward Freddie.

"The boss said they wanted to do an exchange somewhere. Maybe they're taking Freddie's parents there. Wouldn't that be a perfect plan?" Freddie strained to hear the agent's words.

"Yeah, except we've only got two people there for protection. Let's get a move on." Jared's last words faded as the two agents walked away from where Freddie lay on the ground.

Alexander rose and pointed away from the agents. She stood and dusted debris from her clothing before facing her captors. "Why were you heading for the retreat center?"

Chapter Twenty-Six

Kent left the woods and edged along the side of the building. The eerie quiet was unsettling. He bent and picked up a pebble when he reached the corner nearest the front of the retreat center. Tossing the small stone into the open space, he waited for a reaction. When none came, he peered around the side with his gun in a ready position. The scene that greeted him was shocking. The mule stood over two of his agents, poking at them with its long nose.

Kent shouted for help. "Victor, meet me at the front of the house. Use caution. I see two agents down. That crazy mule seems to be hovering over them."

"I'm here, boss, and seeing the same. I'll get the mule out of the way." Victor approached the animal murmuring something soothing. Kent surveyed the surrounding woods while Victor made it to the mule and grabbed the halter. The mule willingly went with the man who'd taken care of him the day before.

Once the mule was away from the fallen agents, Kent ran closer and heard both of his people moaning. Angela rolled off Carlton as Kent leaned over to check her condition.

"My head's killing me." She squinted at Kent. "I'm seeing double images." Her hands wrapped around her belly as she released the contents of her stomach.

"Where is Freddie?" Kent rasped.

"She came out to help me with Carlton. Then..." Angela heaved again as her hands moved to her head.

Kent wanted to throw up himself, but knew he needed to act. First, they needed to assess Carlton's condition and get some emergency help for the two injured agents in front of him. Next in line was his concern for his family and Freddie. He ran to the building and pounded on the door.

"It's Kent, let me in." Seconds that seemed like minutes later, Chelsea opened the door as the children peered around her side. He wrapped his arms around them. "Have you seen Freddie?"

Chelsea shook her head. "We hid when she told us to. Has something happened to her? We thought they were just trying to get Carlton back inside until we heard you holler for the other agent."

Kent gave his family one more hug. "I think they have her. I'm going to call for medical help for Angela and Carlton. You stay locked up."

Chelsea's eyes widened. The children grasped onto the edges of her clothing. He didn't need to tell her who the "they" were, only that Freddie was in trouble. Kent knew his daughter-in-law would protect the children to the best of her ability, but he didn't want to leave them alone in the building.

By the time Victor returned without the mule, Kent had made a decision. "You're going to stay here with the wounded and my family. I'm going to start tracking the crooks, if I can find a trail. Hopefully, Jared and Steve will meet me somewhere between here and there. Then we can surround them before they get to their vehicle."

Victor's mouth opened, as if to protest, but he nodded after looking toward the wounded agents. "Yes, sir."

Kent pulled the two-way radio from his side, praying that Alexander or Marcus didn't hear. "Everyone, this is Kent. Agents Angela and Carlton are down. Perps are on the run with the witness. Sarah, call 9-1-1 and get some medical help to the retreat center. Send Leon to help with security here. You and Bart break camp and drive the RVs to the ranch. If you catch up with Alexander and Marcus on the way down, use caution. I'm tracking Freddie's kidnappers from this end. Steve and Jared, if you see them, follow and we'll have them surrounded once I catch up. Return to radio silence except for an emergency."

He ran to the edge of the property and began scanning for any hints of a trail. It didn't take long to spot where two sets of footprints headed for the woods dragging a third person with smaller feet between them.

"I'm off," Kent shouted.

Chelsea waved from the door where she held up a granola bar and water bottle. "Take these with you. You'll need to keep your strength up."

"Thanks. You do the same for our family." Kent gave her one more hug.

She gave his arm a squeeze. "Be careful. Bring Freddie back to us. She's part of the family too."

"I hope to make that possible when this is all over." Kent stuffed her gifts in the backpack with his other supplies and began his trek. The trail was pretty obvious in most places. Freddie must have remembered to leave hints after their adventure on the mountain. Had it only been days since that had transpired? It was hard to believe, but true.

This time they weren't walking in a group and talking about bears and animal droppings. He was alone. She was with her worst nightmares, Marcus and Alexander. Pushing forward, he concentrated on tracking their steps. A while later, the sound of something rustling through the undergrowth made him pause. Soft voices reached his ears. Male, not female. He stepped behind a large tree and waited to see who was coming nearer.

"How much farther do we need to go? If they followed the same path we're on, we should have run into them based on the time Kent gave his emergency call."

Kent recognized his agent's voice. "I'm over here, Steve. It looks like they took a slightly different trail on their way back. You must have passed them." Frustration wrapped its way around Kent's chest as he came from his hiding place and waved the other agents over. "Help me follow this trail and let's see if we can catch up with them."

They forged ahead until they spotted a large area of flattened plant growth. Kent shook his head. "It looks like you were close enough for them to take cover while you passed by on the other trail."

Jared walked into the woods. "You're right, Boss. The trail we followed is over here. They must have heard us coming and hid."

Kent started tracking the trail again. There were fewer clues other than an occasional bent branch.

Steve followed behind him, speaking in a low voice. "They're headed back to their SUV. I don't think we have time to catch them."

Kent stopped in his tracks and grabbed the radio. "Agent Levigne, are you on?"

Nora responded immediately. "I'm here."

"Good, be ready to follow if you spot the vehicle you saw earlier. Don't try to confront. We need to know where they're going. Is that understood?" Kent started moving down the path as he spoke.

"Yes, sir. I'll be discreet and keep on their tail. Is it safe to leave Tamera alone?"

"I don't think she's in danger anymore. Tell her to stay inside until the agents in the RVs or the medical team arrive. She may need to let the medics use the inner road. Just be ready to roll." Kent attached the radio to his belt and focused on the dwindling trail. He broke into a trot when an engine roared to life in the distance.

~~~~~

"You want to know how we knew where you were." Alexander laughed as he pulled Freddie toward one of the SUVs parked near wildflowers growing at the edge of the road. "Kent's phone number wasn't the only one that Martin helped us keep tabs on. When we noticed many of the local agents' phones were headed for this property, we figured out you were at one of two spots. We got lucky, figuring you'd be hidden away in the woods rather than on the road."

Marcus pushed through the bushes and started following the clearer trail taken by the agents they'd hidden from. "It helped that Martin dated the owner, and she showed him around the whole place. Too bad the authorities captured him and busted our whole ring of conspirators. Thanks to the federals, we just need to grab some money and get away to
~~~~~

some tropical island with immunity. Once you give us Max's code, we'll have plenty of travel money."

Marcus leaned closer. She could smell his sweat mingling with fading cologne. He pulled her through the flowers and pushed her toward the back seat of the vehicle. Several bees swarmed around them. Marcus swatted, stirring the insects into a frenzy. Freddie jerked in pain as the bees used her arm for a pincushion. She thought of the antihistamines sitting back in her room at the retreat center and prayed for a minimal reaction to the sting.

Marcus slid into the seat beside her and sneered. "Want to come with us to our island and have a little fun?"

"No." Freddie leaned away from the threatening man. He laughed and pulled a hunting knife from a sheath attached to his belt. She gulped. He smirked and got back out of the car. He went to the other vehicle and slashed the valve stems on the agent's vehicle's tires. Freddie's hopes deflated with the tires.

"That should keep your boyfriend and his crew busy for a while." Marcus climbed back in beside her while Alexander revved the engine and took off down the road. "Better put your seatbelt on, sweetheart. This might be a wild ride."

Freddie complied but shifted as close to the door as she could in the confined space. Pain drew her attention to her arm. Bright red skin and swelling surrounded where the bee had done its worst. Silence filled the car as they bounced over the rough road that led them to a smoother country route and then to a highway. Marcus leaned against his side of the car and started snoring once the roads smoothed out. Freddie looked up and caught Alexander glancing at her in the rearview mirror.

"Know anybody in a little blue sedan?" Alexander returned to facing the road ahead.

"Not around here. I've only been in SUVs the last week or so. Why do you ask?" Freddie hoped someone had followed them, but a sedan didn't seem like a likely choice for any of the federal agents.

"It's probably just a coincidence, but they seem to be heading the same way we are. I'm going to slow down, and you're going to give me an honest answer if you recognize them. If I think you're lying then that will come out of your parents' well-being. Understood?"

"Yes." She understood all too well.

Alexander slowed the SUV. The woman in the sedan passed them. Her head bobbed to whatever music she seemed to be enjoying as her eyes focused straight ahead. Her jaw moved to either the words of a song or a wad of gum in her mouth.

Freddie sighed. "As much as I wish we were being followed, I am sorry to say, I've never seen that driver before. She doesn't look like a federal agent to me." She slumped back against the seat.

"Good." Alexander sped back up and passed the woman, who did appear headed the same way they were. When Freddie looked back several minutes later, the blue car was a tiny speck in the distance. Help wasn't on the way. Only God could help her now. She closed her eyes and began to plead for His deliverance as she massaged her aching arm.

When she opened her eyes after her brief prayer, she knew exactly where they were. Police tape surrounded the front door of the main office of MAX Enterprises. She knew the building well. Even though she'd only worked there a few years, the place had burned its way into her memories as something she never wanted to see again.

Alexander pulled into the public garage next to the building and parked in a space near the back. Marcus grabbed her arm as soon as they left the car.

Freddie yelped. Pain shot through her arm. "You're hurting me. Bee stings and I don't get along very well."

Marcus just shook his head and led her by the other arm as they headed toward a back entrance to MAX Enterprises. Surprise filled Freddie when they headed downstairs instead of up to her old office.

"Why not go upstairs? I might see something that would remind me of the code you're looking for." The basement had given her the creeps when she was younger.

"First we want to make sure you cooperate. I figure seeing your parents might make you more willing to talk." Marcus pushed her toward the darkened end of a hallway where paper records had once been stored. Surely a cyber-related business had converted everything into electronic documents by now.

A light shone from beneath the padlocked door. A board held in place between two metal brackets helped barricade the door against anyone escaping from inside. Alexander twisted a key in the lock and slid the board to the side. When he opened the entryway, Freddie's dad and stepmom, Lindy, sat in the musty room. She stifled a sneeze as the heavy air reached her nose.

Her parents each wore an ankle bracelet and chains that tethered them to rusty metal shelving filled with haphazardly stacked ancient file boxes. The chains seemed long enough to give them access to a portable potty sitting between them. It looked like no one had bothered to dispose of the old files after all. She recognized her handwriting on the box above Lindy's head.

"Welcome to your parents' home away from home." Marcus pushed her farther into the room.

Lindy stared at Freddie's face and gasped. "What have they done to your arm and neck? They're all red."

Freddie looked down at her limb. The bee stings had swollen and a rash had spread upward. She wasn't feeling any other adverse effects. Maybe she could use her reaction to distract the criminals from their purpose. A little dramatic breathing might do the trick once they released her family. She wrapped her arms around her parents and whispered.

"I love you. I think I'm going to have a—an over-reaction." The words "an over" were mouthed, not even spoken as a whisper.

"Oh, dear." Lindy ran a hand down Freddie's bee stung arm and shook her head. "I hope you don't have a problem this time." Her stepmom's voice sounded too dramatic in Freddie's ears, but she nodded.

Freddie turned back to their captors, holding her arm close to her chest. She put on her best pained expression. "I'm here now. Let them go and I'll give you what you want."

"Not happening. We'll keep them until we have the code for Max's secret bank accounts." Alexander smirked.

"Then you better make it quick." Freddie faked several sharp breaths and placed both hands on her chest. "If this rash spreads anymore, I'm going to need medication that I don't have. The breathing will get worse and I'll probably pass out on you. I suggest you release them before I'm unconscious and unable to give you codes."

She coughed several times into her fist, attempting to sound raspy. A bubble of spit went down her throat the wrong way, sending her into spasmodic wheezing. Trying to catch her breath became real as she choked and couldn't speak. She prayed the reaction didn't become a real one. *Help me, Lord.*

Her father rose. His chains rattled as he moved to Freddie and patted her back. "Why don't you let us all go? Can't you see my daughter needs medical attention? I'll make sure the authorities charge you with murder if something happens to her."

"It wouldn't be the first murder we've arranged." Marcus' laugh was sinister.

"What do you mean by that?" Freddie's voice shook, but she'd cleared her throat enough to rasp the words out.

"Let's just say Max was an easy target. You people are sitting ducks." Marcus smirked.

"This sitting duck has no plans to give you what you want if that's the way you want to play it." Freddie took a stance between her parents and the threatening men.

"Breathing better?" Alexander snorted and raised an eyebrow.

Freddie swallowed. She'd forgotten to keep the act up. She held up her appendage which now had a bright red rash from wrist to shoulder. "Do you think I can fake this?" She dismissed the slight hitch in her breathing. Her head swam. Too much stress was getting to her.

Alexander shrugged. "I suggest you start spilling the codes or we'll start working on some painful experiences for your old man."

Marcus pulled the knife from its holder and rubbed it on his pants leg. "Looks like Papa could use a shave."

Chapter Twenty-Seven

Kent paced as he waited for Victor to arrive with the SUV they'd left at the retreat center. Leon would stay to protect Kent's family at the cabin. Notification that a helicopter ambulance airlifted Angela and Carlton to the hospital relieved his concern over their conditions. He, Steve, and Jared had ridden to the ranch in the RVs, after they'd abandoned their flat-tired vehicle along the road. Sarah and Bart were inside the ranch house with Tamera and would stay with her for the time being.

As he looked up the trail toward the retreat center, a cloud of dust became visible. Good, their wait was over. Now they just had to find where Alexander and Marcus had taken Freddie.

His phone rang. He was glad to be back in a cell reception area. He recognized Agent Levigne's number. "Kent here. Do you have an update?"

"I followed them to MAX Enterprises Headquarters. They're somewhere in the building. I've parked a few blocks away. Do you want me to enter the building?" Agent Levigne's heavy breathing seemed to indicate she was running.

"Wait for backup. We'll be there in an hour, but it wouldn't hurt to get the police involved right now. Don't try to do anything by yourself. Call 9-1-1 and observe until you have help. That's an order." Kent ended the conversation and headed for the SUV.

Kent, Jared, and Steve crowded into the vehicle Victor drove. "Take us to MAX Enterprises Headquarters. Agent Levigne just called to let me know she followed them there. They've taken Freddie inside the offices." Kent snapped his seatbelt in place.

Victor put the SUV in gear as the others buckled up. "I'll run the emergency vehicle lights so we can get there faster."

"Good. I've asked Agent Levigne to inform local law enforcement. She'll stand down until assistance arrives. All Nora knows is that they are somewhere in the building." Kent hoped the woman would follow his orders.

"Do you think Freddie's parents are there also?" Kent's shoulder rammed the side of the SUV as Victor took the vehicle around a sharp turn. "The crooks might be using them as leverage to get what they want."

"I suspect they are, based on the trail I followed. Freddie seemed to be dragging her feet up to a point and then there were fewer clues. I'm guessing they said something that made her more cooperative. Earlier this week, she pretty much admitted to being willing to make the ultimate sacrifice for her family." Kent looked out the window at the blurred scenery. He prayed for her safety and started thinking about plans for rescuing Freddie and her loved ones. He lifted his phone and dialed his secretary.

"Hey, Dianne, do you have access to a floor plan for MAX Enterprises? Alexander and Marcus have Freddie somewhere in that building."

"I'll do my best to find one and text it to you. Anything else?" The click of Dianne's nimble fingers on a computer keyboard rattled in the background.

"That should do for now. Thanks. Wait. I'd appreciate your prayers." He knew they needed all the prayers they could find.

"I'm praying right now, Boss," Dianne replied.

"I always knew you could do two things at once. I appreciate you." Kent signed off. Life was too short not to thank those around him. He glanced at the men in the car. "Have I ever thanked you guys for all you do for the department and me?"

"Are you getting soft on us, Boss? Miss Freddie has brought out your kinder side." Victor's comment brought chuckles from Steve and Jared.

"We're praying too." Steve spoke as Jared and Victor nodded.

A ping drew Kent's attention back to his phone. Dianne had sent a scan of the floor plans. It didn't look like much had changed since he'd been in the building as Freddie's boyfriend. He'd met her there several times, but then she'd started insisting they connect at other places. He should have picked up on something being off-base then, but love had blinded him. Today he'd go in with his eyes wide open, unless the police had taken care of rescuing Freddie before they arrived.

Fifteen minutes later, he checked the time and wondered why Nora hadn't called back since her initial contact. Dialing her number proved fruitless. Why wasn't she answering? He searched the internet and located the local number for the city's police station and called them.

"Hello. This is Federal Agent Kent Russell. I'm checking to make sure you received a call to go to MAX Enterprises."

"Yes, sir. We have the building surrounded, but we haven't made contact with the agent who made the initial report or the people who are supposed to be inside. All seems quiet at the moment. When we tried to call the agent back, she didn't answer our call. The police on scene are wondering if it was a hoax."

"This isn't a hoax. There is a hostage situation going on in the building. Two perps, Alexander Johnson and Marcus Stanley, are holding a federal witness named Winifred Grimsley and possibly her parents. Both Johnson and Stanley have warrants for their arrests. My team will be there as soon as we can. Keep the area surrounded."

"Will do. Our negotiator is due to arrive on scene in the next few minutes." The policewoman's words assured him they would follow through.

Kent hesitated before mentioning the agent who might have gone where he asked her not to go. He chose his words carefully. "As far as contacting my missing agent, I'm having the same problem. I hope the crooks didn't discover her presence. That would complicate things even more."

"Understood. What time should I tell our officers to expect you?"

"We should be there before the top of the hour." Kent closed the call and urged Victor to drive faster.

When they arrived, flashing lights from police cars and ambulances surrounded MAX Enterprises. Darkness encompassed the structure. No interior lighting showed through the windows. No one had responded to the negotiator's calls to phone lines inside or to loud megaphone announcements.

Kent's thoughts turned to the floor plan he'd studied. There was a basement filled with storage rooms. Maybe they were in one of them.

"Let's go in through the basement entrance in the back. We'll see what we can find down there before working our way through the upper stories of the building."

The police detective in charge agreed and sent in a team prepared to bust open doors ahead of a joint force that would work together for the arrests. As they approached the back entrance, Kent heard a moan from bushes near the door. He held out a hand for everyone to stop. "Who's there?"

"Help." Nora's faint voice barely reached him. He parted the bushes and saw her lying on the ground. Blood covered her shirt.

"What happened?"

"I saw them..." Nora's eyes rolled as she passed out.

Kent waved to one of the local policemen. "Go get the medics to help her. The rest head inside with me."

They stepped into a long hallway and busted the first door open. Nothing. Then Kent heard people calling out. They followed the sound to the far end of the hallway. Kent spotted a doorway held closed with a wooden board and brackets. He removed those but a lock still held the entry closed.

"Step aside. We're coming in."

The police battering ram pounded on the entry until the frame busted loose. Kent stepped into the room.

"Thank the Lord, you're here." Stepmom Lindy Grimsley sat chained in place. Blood dripped from Mr. Grimsley's neck. It looked like someone had been cutting gashes into his skin. Kent scanned the room for the others.

"Where's Freddie?" Kent's fist tightened as sweat formed on his brow.

"They took her. She started breathing too fast and told them they wouldn't get any codes until she was treated for her bee sting," Lindy answered.

Freddie's dad wheezed. "She's never had a reaction that bad before. I hope they took her to a hospital." He needed medical treatment too.

"How long ago did they leave?" Kent asked.

"It was before we heard the sirens." Tears filled Lindy's eyes. "We hoped they had called an ambulance."

Kent rushed from the building. He needed to find Freddie.

~~~~~

A warm hand patted Freddie's wrist as she fought to open her eyes. "Welcome back, ma'am. You've had a rough go of it, but I see you're waking up."

The female attached to the hands and voice smelled of disinfectant and soap. Faint sounds of pinging and beeping came from beyond the curtains surrounding her small cubicle. They must have made it to an ER before all her breathing cut off. She had a hazy memory of being with Alexander and Marcus before she blacked out going down the basement hallway at MAX Enterprises. She still felt woozy but tried to say something to the woman in scrubs. Her attempt at speaking must not have been coherent. The nurse shook her head and raised her palms as she shrugged.

She hovered close again. "Try not to make sense of anything." The blonde woman laid a warmed blanket over Freddie. "We've given you a powerful dose of epinephrine and some antihistamines. You're going to be sleepy for a while. I'll let your husband and brother know you're waking up."

She had no husband or brother. Those crooks had lied to the hospital or clinic or wherever she was. Freddie snapped her eyes closed and pretended to sleep. She felt like she hovered in a zombie-like state, so it was only half an act. Alexander's strong cologne floated in the air as she heard the curtains open and then draw closed. He tapped on her side. She moaned and wrapped the covers tighter around her. She muttered what she hoped sounded like, "Go away."

"Just give me the numbers and we'll get out of here." The stench of onion breath combined with his cologne made her sneeze.

Freddie thought back to the transistor on Max's desk and some of the other numbers she'd gone over. Her tongue seemed to tangle as she muttered out several of the possible codes she'd discussed with Kent. She hoped he was safe and coming after her soon.
~~~~~

Alexander whipped out his phone and started searching. Freddie rolled to her side and watched his attempts through bleary eyes. She yawned and pulled the warm covering over her shoulders. This might take a while. Alexander's face turned a brighter red with each unsuccessful try. She wanted to remind him that she had no codes, but figured those words would make his anger worse.

Marcus leaned into the room. Unpleasant body odor filled the space. "What's taking so long? Someone's liable to find that agent I stabbed, and this hospital will be swarming with cops if you don't hurry."

Voices in the next cubical quieted. The nurse's call button rang from that room and in the nurse's station. Once the nurse responded, a whispered conversation took place with the room's occupants. A code went out over the hospital intercom soon after. The noise made Freddie's head pound.

"Try again, Winifred, and don't be wrong this time." Alexander clasped his fingers around her neck. "I won't be saving your life if you get it wrong this time."

Freddie gulped as her fingers searched for her own nurse's button. "Try Max's office extension, MAXE."

"That isn't a number."

"It is if you're looking at a phone keypad. That translates to 6-2-9-3." Freddie sagged back into the comfort of her pillow when he released her neck. Her fingers connected with the call button. At the same time Alexander's phone started emitting a loud noise with the notification blasting out, "You've been hacked by MAX Enterprises."

She pushed the nurse's button as he ran from the room. At least those two were on the run without Max's hidden cash. She prayed they wouldn't come back asking for more codes that she didn't have. After she explained about being a kidnap victim and the nurse called the police, she closed her eyes and fell into a deep sleep.

Chapter Twenty-Eight

Kent ran for the SUV with Victor and Jared trailing behind him. Steve had agreed to stay with Mr. and Mrs. Grimsley while they sorted out details with the police. He had a good team who knew what to do. Maybe he could talk Jared and Angela into transferring to Ohio. Then again, he might retire and find something safer if he found Freddie agreeable to a future together. He took the passenger seat as Victor settled into the driver's position.

"Where to, Boss? Mercy General or First Medical?" Victor started the engine and looked at Kent.

"Mercy is closer by a minute. Let's head there first." Kent gripped the arm rest. Had he made the right choice? Mercy had been the hospital where his wife passed away from her cancer. Going there again would remind him of a time of sadness. Maybe finding Freddie safe would change his memories of the place. Strobing lights lit the doors to the hospital as they pulled into the ER area. Kent opened the car door when two men raced from the ER and jumped into a dark SUV.

"It's them." Kent put his seat belt back on. "Give chase. I'll call for backup." He dialed 9-1-1. "This is Federal Agent Kent Russell. We're in pursuit of the suspects involved in the kidnapping case at MAX Enterprises earlier this evening. We're leaving Mercy General and headed east on Starling Street. Please advise any patrol cars to assist. The kidnap victim may be at Mercy. Someone needs to check the status of Freddie, I mean, Winifred Grimsley."

Victor rode close to the bumper of the other vehicle and gave it a tap. The reaction of the other driver was to speed up. It was too dangerous to do much more than that as they drove through neighborhood streets. They zigzagged around multiple city blocks until the other car picked up speed and raced down Rocky Bottom Road. Kent remembered the road led to a private airfield where MAX Enterprises and other companies housed their corporate jets.

He called the police again. "They're headed for the airport on Rocky Bottom Road. Can you assist?"

"We'll contact the airfield and send reinforcements ASAP. May we contact you at this number?"

"Yes." Kent braced as Victor edged their vehicle close another time.

Alexander and Marcus' SUV shot forward, leaving them struggling to keep up.

"He must have some kind of turbocharged engine in that thing." Victor shook his head as he floored the gas pedal.

By the time they arrived at the airfield, Alexander and Marcus were climbing into a small idling jet with MAX Enterprises written on the tail. Operating lights gave evidence the plane was ready for flight. Victor pulled the SUV to a stop and popped the trunk.

"There are long-distance weapons in the back, Boss."

Kent grabbed a rifle and checked it for bullets. He lifted the gun to his shoulder and checked the aim. "The time has come to take down a bird in flight."

They rushed to the edge of the runway where the small jet started pulling away. Kent released the safety and held the gun to his shoulder. *Time to put years of gun training into practice...* He took aim and hit one of the tires. The plane skittered to one side. Pointing the gun at the tail he managed to make one of the flaps dangle by a corner. He took out the back wheel next. The plane wouldn't be going anywhere today.

The plane's door opened with lowered stairs. Alexander and Marcus climbed from the plane and started running. The pilot remained in the doorway with his hands up.

"Stop running," Kent shouted. When they kept going, he fired a warning shot over their heads. Both froze and raised their hands. Sirens sounded in the distance and then drew closer.

Police cruisers surrounded the airfield as Kent and Victor cuffed the men's hands behind their backs. Jared read them their rights. He stayed behind to share details with the police and interview the pilot. Once they'd placed Alexander and Marcus in police custody for safekeeping, Kent asked Victor to take him back to the hospital. He needed to find Freddie and make sure she was unharmed.

Arriving at the hospital, he approached the front desk and demanded to know where Freddie was.

"I'm sorry, sir. I have no evidence of her admittance. Her name doesn't appear in the computer or on any paperwork." The woman's firm voice implied she'd given him her final answer.

"She has to be here. I saw the men who brought her here fleeing from this hospital." Kent flashed his re-issued badge and headed to the ER entrance.

The front desk receptionist frowned, but didn't stop Kent. He had a feeling she'd dealt with law enforcement before and his badge had passed the woman's test.

After peeking into several curtained rooms and embarrassing himself and the people inside, he headed to the nurse's station. "I'm looking for a woman in her fifties who was admitted with an anaphylactic response to a bee sting. Her name is Winifred Grimsley. Two men would have come in with her. They may have registered her under a false name. I need to know if she is okay."

One of the nurses glanced at him. "She was one of my patients."

"Was? Did she..." He couldn't finish his question as his heart felt like a lead weight in his chest.

"Sorry, sir. She was under my care during the shift I just finished. Someone from the next shift is working with her for now." She shook her head before continuing.

"We had quite a scare when those two men started talking about stabbing someone. When the one guy's phone started shrieking out a warning about being hacked, they took off running and left the lady behind. They told us her name was Jane Smith, but I'm willing to guess she is your Winifred. She's sleeping off her medication at the moment. She'll be fine once she's more alert." The nurse directed him to the last room on the right.

Kent stepped into the room and sat beside the bed, admiring the woman he'd come to love again. Their young love had been dramatic and fun. He looked forward to a more mature love filled with happiness and satisfaction as they grew old together. He took her soft hand in his and whispered her name.

A smile crossed her lips. "I love you, Kent." She still sounded drugged and he wondered if she realized what she'd said.

He'd take the chance she meant every word. "I love you too. Have you ever thought about retiring from teaching? I'm thinking strongly about my own retirement in the near future. We could take a trip to Paris together for a honeymoon. Then you could travel the world as Winnie Gee and I'd be your protective service guy."

"Mmmm. That sounds nice. Though I think one of us would have to keep a day job. Being an author and illustrator doesn't pay that well." She rolled over to meet his gaze. Her eyes widened. "Was that a proposal?"

"It sure was. Would you like a kiss?" Kent lowered his face closer to hers.

"I sure would." She smiled as her eyes fluttered shut.

He gathered her in his arms and gave her a long kiss.

"Mmm. You taste like a granola bar."

"Your future daughter-in law wanted me to have enough strength to find you."

"You're making me hungry for more."

He pulled her close again and gave her another flavored kiss.

They sighed at the same time and then broke into laughter when Victor pulled back the curtain. He promptly bowed out of the room.

Epilogue

Freddie's arm trembled as her dad stood by her, facing the aisle leading to the front of the church. His voice spoke to her heart as he whispered in her ear.

"I never thought I'd get the chance to walk you down the aisle, but here we are, getting ready to take the steps toward your life as a married woman."

"I'm glad you're here, Dad. I am sorry for all the years you had to be in hiding. It's good to be back in Forest Glen at the church where I grew up. I wish Mom could be here, but Lindy's been an amazing addition to our family."

Freddie ran a hand down the silky material of her wedding dress. Her mother had given Freddie the outfit before she passed away. It hadn't taken much for Lindy to adjust the fit of the gown. The woman was a wonder with a needle and thread.

"Lindy's kept me on the straight and narrow." Her dad chuckled. "Kent is going to have his work cut out for him to keep you in line."

Freddie laughed and straightened her train trailing behind the dress when the pianist started playing "Pachelbel's Canon in D." Stepping down the aisle toward her future husband filled her with joy. Though too old to have children of her own, she could now claim Kent's family as hers.

Freddie would miss teaching her students but had decided that an art lesson would be part of each Winnie Gee book presentation. She'd also arranged to teach weekend art lessons at Amber's art studio. One of her first author presentations would take place at two of her old school buildings in Lee County. Her friend, Rick, was taking care of her Lee County cottage. She would keep it as a writing retreat for herself and as an affordable rental for carefully screened authors or illustrators who needed short breaks from the world.

Kent had retired from his federal job and decided to take over a local security company, providing protective services for events in nearby cities and bodyguards for well-known people who might visit their area. Carlton was his first hire and they all hoped the job would boost the younger man's confidence while providing an income.

Kent planned to be her personal security when she went on tour as Winnie Gee. That is, after their honeymoon. Her heart fluttered. She'd never dreamed of going on a honeymoon. The smell of fresh roses filled the air as Melissa marched ahead of them scattering the aisle with pink and red petals. Her new grandsons shared the duty of carrying pillows holding the wedding rings as they made their way down the lacy runner. Ushers Jared and Steve had unrolled the white path, after making sure everyone had a seat.

Her dad kissed her cheek, drawing her wandering thoughts to focus on her love for Kent as he took her hands in his. Her bouquet awkwardly quivered between their hands. Her mouth dropped open when she remembered she was supposed to pass the white roses to Chelsea, her matron of honor. Angela and her friend Mary, from Lee County, smiled briefly from their positions in the wedding party as she turned the flowers over to her new daughter-in-law. Freddie had chosen lavender for the women's dresses as a tribute to her late mother. Lachlan and agents Victor and Carlton stood beyond Kent, lending their support to the couple as groomsmen wearing classic black tuxedos.

They spoke vows, prayed, lit candles, and then Freddie's heart overflowed with love when Kent kissed her for the first time as husband and wife. A new life full of joy, hope, and adventures awaited them. They walked down the aisle and out the door to where Tamera waited with a carriage pulled by a team of horses. Their ride to the reception hall was too short as they rested in each other's arms and shared meaningful kisses.

"I love you." Their voices spoke in unison. They laughed and shared one more kiss as they faced their future.

The End

MEET THE AUTHOR

Bettie Boswell has always loved to read and write. That interest helped her create musicals for both church and school students. After retiring from thirty-three years of teaching, she decided to write and illustrate stories to share with the world. Her writing interests extend from works for children to adults and from fiction to non-fiction. At the time of this writing she has seven children's books. ***Hidden Witness*** is her fifth novel and second Christian romantic suspense for adults. Her other novels are contemporary and split-time Christian romances. She has written other works for the education market, magazine articles, and contributed to lesson plan collections, devotionals, Guideposts story collections, and short story anthologies. She is a minister's wife, church musician, mother of two grown men, and a grandma. She loves the arts and shares her doodles, and photography from her daily walks, on social media.

MY THANKS

Many thanks to my readers and also to the critique partners who helped make this possible: Ann Cavera, Mary Vee, Kathy McKinsey, Jennifer Dodrill, and Dave Arp. A huge thanks to Tamera L. Kraft and Michelle Levigne at Mt. Zion Ridge Press for their work and encouragement.

To Lee County Virginia Schools. Thank you for allowing me to start my public school teaching career as one of your roving elementary music teachers many years ago. I served three schools, ate a car-window toasted cheese sandwich in my vehicle between buildings, and learned how to straighten out the curves on a few mountain roads to make it to my next stop. Your children were the best singers!

THANK YOU!

Thank you for reading this book from Mt. Zion Ridge Press.

If you enjoyed the experience, learned something, gained a new perspective, or made new friends through story, could you do us a favor and write a review on Goodreads or wherever you bought the book?

Thanks! We and our authors appreciate it.

We invite you to visit our website, MtZionRidgePress.com, and explore other titles in fiction and non-fiction. We always have something coming up that's new and off the beaten path.

And please check out our podcast, **Books on the Ridge,** where we chat with our authors and give them a chance to share what was in their hearts while they wrote their book, as well as fun anecdotes and glimpses into their lives and experiences and the writing process. And we always discuss a very important topic: *Tea!*

You can listen to the podcast on our website or find it at most of the usual places where podcasts are available online. Please subscribe so you don't miss a single episode!

Thanks for reading. We hope you come back soon!

www.ingramcontent.com/pod-product-compliance
Lightning Source LLC
Chambersburg PA
CBHW010611310726
48969CB00010B/2659